FLUTTER OF A
Broken Heart

by Andrea Stryker

PAGE PUBLISHING, INC.
New York, NY

First originally published by Page Publishing, Inc. 2017

ISBN 978-1-63568-668-5 (Paperback)
ISBN 978-1-63568-669-2 (Digital)

Printed in the United States of America

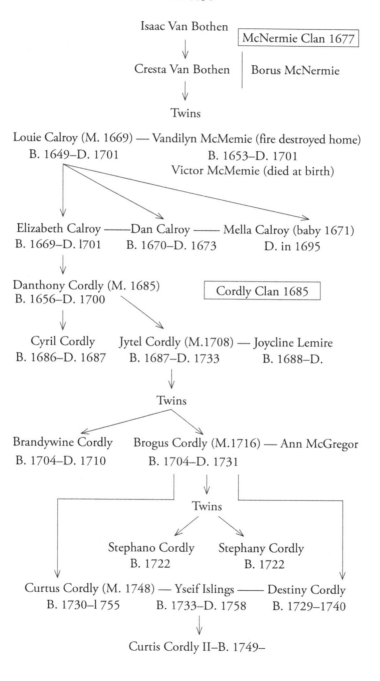

Van Bothen Clan
1614–1656

Isaac Van Bothen

McNermie Clan 1677

Cresta Van Bothen | Borus McNermie

Twins

Louie Calroy (M. 1669) — Vandilyn McMemie (fire destroyed home)
B. 1649–D. 1701   B. 1653–D. 1701
                              Victor McMemie (died at birth)

Elizabeth Calroy ——Dan Calroy —— Mella Calroy (baby 1671)
B. 1669–D. l701   B. 1670–D. 1673   D. in 1695

Danthony Cordly (M. 1685)
B. 1656–D. 1700   Cordly Clan 1685

Cyril Cordly   Jytel Cordly (M.1708) — Joycline Lemire
B. 1686–D. 1687   B. 1687–D. 1733   B. 1688–D.

Twins

Brandywine Cordly   Brogus Cordly (M.1716) — Ann McGregor
B. 1704–D. 1710   B. 1704–D. 1731

Twins

Stephano Cordly   Stephany Cordly
B. 1722   B. 1722

Curtus Cordly (M. 1748) — Yseif Islings —— Destiny Cordly
B. 1730–l755   B. 1733–D. 1758   B. 1729–1740

Curtis Cordly II–B. 1749–

CHAPTER

one

Laura walked down the cobblestone street. Her arms were crossed in front of her to keep the damp, chilled night air from making her colder than she already was. Thinking to herself, "Why did I leave the sunny warmth of California for this?" She knew already what it was to run, and run away she did from the thing or the feeling that has haunted her since her mother's death.

She was almost eighteen when the accident happened, and her life has never been the same since going into the hospital late on a Friday night after the phone call telling her that her mother had been involved in a hit and run and that she was in the ICU in Cobbles Memorial Hospital. That wasn't the hard part. The hard part was getting there and the doctors telling her as she looked at her mom with all the tubes and machines hooked up to her that she was brain dead and the only thing that was keeping her here were the machines. Then the question was asked, "Does she have a DNR [Do Not Resuscitate order]?" It was Laura's decision whether or not to pull the plug. Could she really do it, knowing her mother would never wake up, never smile or kiss her goodnight ever again?

She told the doctor that night that she would give them her answer in the morning and reluctantly they agreed.

She sat there with her head entwined with her mom's and cried. She asked out loud the question most on her mind, "Momma, would you want me to do this if it was me on this bed and not you? Would you do the same?"

Laura fell asleep holding onto her mom's hand, sitting at her hospital bedside, but it was not a good sleep because just as soon as her eyes were closed and the breathing slowed, visions started to show up in her mind.

It was her standing in a house that she did not recognize, but could have sworn she had seen in some old pictures her mom had in the photo album. Feeling as if she was not alone in this dream house, Laura began to look around the room and started to see her surroundings.

The wallpaper with the fan-type designs, window curtains that were heavy in color and fabric, and the furniture that was oversized for the small room. What really caught her attention was the television set. It was one that you had to get up to turn the channel, and sitting on the top of it were a pair of antenna, the kind people called rabbit ears. She thought to herself, "They don't make televisions like this anymore. This is 2009."

Still standing where she was, a feeling as if she was being watched began to invade into her bones, but there was no one in the room with her. Looking to her left, Laura saw a staircase that went up to the next level and she started to walk over to the stairs. The closer she got to them, the more that feeling came to her, but she just shrugged it off as it was a creepy dream and placed her hand onto the staircase banister. In that moment she heard a loud yelling, then the sounds of screams coming from one of the bedrooms.

When she took her hands off the bannister, the sounds stopped. Laura could not believe what had just happened, so she tried again. This time there were no screams. Nothing. Thinking it was her head playing tricks on her, she climbed, carefully trying not to put too much weight on each step. At first she thought she might fall right through. Up one, up two, up three, up four. This one creaked and moaned as she stopped down so she lightly put her foot closer toward the wall to help ease the weight. Up she went until she was about five steps from the top of the staircase, and not thinking, she put her hand on the bannister again.

Swoosh! She immediately heard the screams again, but this time she also heard the sounds of someone running. All this was in a split second of time because as soon as Laura touched it, she pulled her hand away, but it was too late.

The screams were closer now. When she looked up the hallway, there were shadows from under one of the four doors that lined the walls. Hesitating, Laura did not want to go farther, but she is a curious type and lifted her legs to walk the last few steps. In her ears there were whistles, beeps, and the sounds of voices as if they were on top of her.

A touch on her shoulder woke her, and opening her eyes, reality gave her a cold slap. Nurses, doctors, and people in white-colored clothes were all around. One was telling her that she had to leave the room while they worked on the patient. Moments felt like forever while Laura waited, then she heard the one sound no one wanted to hear, a long beeeeeep and nothing else.

Mom was dead! The doctor came out with a saddened but well-practiced look and said, "Ms. Wilds, I am very sorry. We just could not save her." Putting his hand on her shoulder as if to comfort her, he squeezed and walked on. Standing, watching all the others leave, she just watched as if frozen in time.

CHAPTER

two

Blinking, Laura could not believe that she had walked almost fifteen blocks while she thought once again of her mom. "I've got to stop doing that. One of these days I am going to fall in to an open manhole!" Chuckling, she realized she had said this out loud. She hoped no one was watching her talk to herself. Really feeling the cold and dampness of early morning, Laura was glad to round the last corner of the block that her flat was on.

She reached into the left pocket of her jeans and grabbed the only key she had, the one to her front door. While she was getting ready to open her door, she looked up the road toward her place and stopped. Looking at her place with a question and fright she realized she didn't remember leaving any lights on. She slowly and cautiously walked closer. Still feeling as if someone or something was watching her, she really wanted to go into her home, but with the lights on and knowing she had shut them off, she gave it a second thought. "Mmmm, I wonder if Jamie is still up and if he will go in to the flat with me." She entered the hallway, but didn't go up the stairs to her own place. Instead she passed them and, just below, rang Jamie's bell. "Brrring, Brrring," the twisty bell chimed. Laura paused, then readied to ring again when she heard the sound of stumbling and perhaps a bit of cursing from the other side of the door.

Smiling, because she knew now he was awake from her ringing the bell, Laura braced herself. The door opened and between the door jam and the door, attached by a chain lock was a young pimply faced kid with shiny braces on his teeth. He looked really pissed off. "Who the hell is it? Don't you know what fucking time it is?" The words didn't fit the face, and Laura said softly, "Jamie, it's me Laura. I think someone is in my apartment because the lights are on. Will you come with me to check it out?"

Breathing in, Jamie unlocked the chain and opened the door. "Shit, Lar, I'm sorry. You said what about what lights?"

Repeating herself, she told him that she knew she had shut them off when leaving earlier and now they were on. "Will you come with me?"

Lighting a cigarette, he took a drag and replied, "Guess so, I'm fucking up now, no offense," as he inhaled the smoke. "Hold on, let me put my shoes on."

Laura has known Jamie for about a year now since she transferred from California to London for her schooling. She couldn't take the memories from California anymore.

"Okay, Laura, let's go find this bad man who turns lights on in other people's homes."

"You are really a jerk, Jamie, you know that?" she replied.

He just gave a smile and a puff of smoke to her. "Gimme your key," he said as they started up the stairs. *Creak, creak, creak.* The stairs gave away anyone who walked on them.

"Did you hear anyone go up?" she asked.

"No, I just got in a while ago myself, sorry," he replied.

As they topped the stairs, Laura started to get that creepy feeling again but didn't say anything. She just grabbed onto the back pocket of Jamie's pants ahead of her. Looking at his pants, she thought, *If he wasn't such a geekie jerk, he really does have a nice ass and a kickin' bod!*

Oh, bad girl, her brain told her.

Jamie put his ear to the door first to hear if anyone was still inside, holding his finger over his lips as if to say "shhh." Hearing no sounds, he took the key and put it into the lock. He opened the door in a smooth shoving motion that really didn't fit his looks. "Aye ya," he said as if trying to be a bad ass, then going into the flat and making a leap with a loud "gotcha!" as he entered the TV room and then the bedroom area.

"Nope, no one here," he said, "but whoever it was, was looking for something because they left it a mess."

Laura, who had stayed outside the door while he "did his thing" as she called it, walked in and couldn't believe her eyes. The kitchen had no cabinet left closed. Pots and pans and even the stove was opened wide. Turning into the TV room, there was nothing untouched. There were books on the floor, the couch was turned over, and what looked like knife marks in the upholstery.

"What the hell, Laura?" Jamie said without thinking. "They managed to really do a number on your things but left your bedroom alone? That's really weird. You calling the cops?"

"You betcha," said Laura. "My insurance won't cover anything if I don't. Stay with me until they get here, please?"

"Kay-O, Lar. Only for you but then I'm going back to sleep. A guy needs his beauty sleep, no?" said Jamie.

Laura smiled back at him. Going to the wall to find the outlet to the telephone, because with all the mess, she didn't see the phone itself. She traced the line and found it laying under a large stack of books over by the window. Hanging up the receiver for a few seconds, then picking it up to her ear, hearing a dial tone, she pushed 999.

"Nine nine nine emergency, can I help you?" a gentleman said in a long English way.

"Yes, my place has been broken into and all my stuff has been ransacked. He or they even cut up my furniture!" Laura said. The operator verified her address and she asked him to send someone quickly, then she hung up and waited.

Jamie had lit another cigarette and, not seeing the ash tray, held his hand out and flicked the ashes into it. "That's gross. Let me find you something," she said. She came back from the kitchen with a small glass with a little water in it and handed it to him. "I wonder why they didn't do anything to my bedroom," she asked Jamie.

He hunched his shoulders as if to say "I don't know" but said nothing. They heard the sound of sirens—"nerrdo, nerrdo, wapp, wapp, nerrdo, nerrdo"—now closer with the last sound of "yerp" as the noise stopped but the lights were still on as they went down to meet them.

The one driving got out and asked if she was the person who called and Laura said, "Yes. I'm Laura Wilds and this is my neighbor from downstairs, Jamie."

As they spoke, another officer got out and, putting his cap on and pulling up his pants said, "How bad is it?"

Laura said, "They wrecked my place!"

"Now, Ms. Wilds, let's go have a look," the first one said and they went on up. As the officers entered, the kitchen was what they saw first. The one officer looked at the other and told him, "Go get the kit, bring the camera too, and call the station to tell them we need the investigator here for prints."

He exited to make the call and the first one stopped and said, "I'm Officer Blakely and the other is Shamble. We will see what we can do here, but do you have somewhere else to stay tonight or maybe for a few nights?"

Laura looked at Jamie who already knew then she was going to ask him because she really didn't know anybody else yet. He said to the police officer, "She can stay with me." Looking back at her and now trying to be funny, he said, "As long as I don't find any panties hanging from my shower ring."

Laura smiled and said angrily but laughing too, "I don't hang my panties, thank you very much! Asshole!"

The cop just smiled and chuckled a bit. "You will have to wait until we get done here before you can take anything out."

"They didn't move anything in my bedroom. Can I get some clothes and my books for school?" Laura asked.

"Let me look first," the officer said. He went into the room and, taking his hat off as if puzzled and scratching his head, thought, *Well, this is strange.* He said yes but wanted to let them photograph the place first, then they could have it as it was.

"Thanks," Laura replied.

C H A P T E R
three

Time passed quickly once everyone got there. It was now almost 7:30 a.m. Laura had to be at school by nine so she went down and took a "quickie" shower, dressed, and told Jamie thanks for letting her stay. She would be back after class but now she was off to catch the bus. All morning her mind was not on school, but the apartment and yet she stuck it out until two. Then she was on her way back to the house by bus.

Arriving there, she walked up to the entrance door and it looked like it did any other day, but when she entered and looked up, there was yellow police tape all over her apartment door with the words "Do Not Enter, Police Investigation" in bold red letters. Loudly Laura said, "Fuck! This is not going to be good!"

Standing there alone while knocking on Jamie's door, a chill came down her spine and, again, the feeling of being watched. Hearing the locks, she quickly looked around and up to the second level but no one was there. She was thinking she was nuts, so she just brushed it off again as being odd.

"Hey there, roomie," Jamie said jokingly with a big smile on his mouth. She went in.

Sitting on the chair looking out to nothing she asked, "Why did they do this? I don't have anything of value. Hell. I don't even carry cash on me!"

"Maybe you have something that you don't know is worth a lot of dough. I don't know!"

"No, the only thing I have is this necklace that my mom wore all the time, and when she died, I took it to keep her close to me. She never even took it off as long back as I can remember," Laura replied.

"Maybe that's it then. Only they didn't know that you wear it," he said.

"I don't think it has any value," she answered. "My mom did say once that her mother gave it to her when she was really young and told her never to take it off. She said that her mother, my grandma, was really superstitious."

"Was she from the States?" Jamie asked.

"No, I think she was from Germany or Russia or someplace like that," she said.

"Well, it might be worth something then. Maybe you should check it out."

"Later," she said. "I'm hungry. Wanna go get something to eat?"

Jamie replied, "Naw, you go ahead. I'm gonna get some more sleep."

Grabbing her coat because she was not going to get caught freezing her butt off again, Laura left the loft and started to walk the street down to the little pizza joint a few blocks away. When walking, she started to get that creepy feeling again. She started to look around at the few people that were out. There was a man and woman holding hands like they were married, a young kid with some books, a woman pushing a baby carriage (the kid screaming as she walked), and farther down the street, a guy. Just a guy standing alone. Not actually acting like he was waiting on someone or having someplace to go, but just standing there. Laura thought that was strange.

She reached for the necklace that was around her neck, not even knowing she was doing it because it had become a habit. Laura rubbed the locket with her thumb as if to comfort herself. This time as she walked and rubbed, a voice came into her head, "You are just as pretty as your mother and grandmother."

Startled, she let go of the necklace and stopped to look around. No one was any different on the street except...Wait...The man standing by himself was gone.

CHAPTER
four

Okay, that was weird, Laura thought, but her stomach started to really growl at her now. She walked on only now really keeping her eyes open and watching the people around her. She rounded the corner and saw the pizza place with all its lights on and people inside. Laura walked just a bit faster because, where there was light and people, there was safety—at least she hoped so. Grabbing the door and pulling it open, she immediately smelled the odor of dough, tomatoes, and the sweet smell of pizza. Her stomach really made her want everything on the menu but Mom always said, "Never go grocery shopping or into a restaurant on an empty stomach. You will buy things you won't ever eat."

So looking at the menu, Laura ordered a small pie with cheese and sausage, a large salad, and a six pack of beer and took the order ticket. She got out of line and saw an open seat at the table near the window so she went and sat down.

Just sitting down and taking a sip of the cup of beer she ordered for the wait, she looked out the window. Across the roadway standing under the street light was that same strange guy she had seen on her way here. *No way, it can't be. That's the same guy*, she thought. This time she could see what he looked like. He was tall, about six foot to six two, with dark hair that hang to his shoulders. His face was very strong and chiseled. He could have come right off the cover of one of those Romance novels because the long trench coat he was wearing didn't leave anything to the imagination.

Mmmm, Laura thought.

"Number nineteen," a loud voice was heard saying and she was brought out of the night dream she had been in.

"Shit," Laura said under her voice. Getting up and out of the chair, she couldn't help but taking a glance back to the light post. *I knew it was too good to be true*, she thought. Paying for the order and grabbing the bag, she ventured back to Jamie's flat to eat.

CHAPTER
five

She thought how empty the streets had gotten in just a short time but was not really worried about it. "Mmmph" was all she said. The walk back was pretty boring with no one out. Getting up the stairs and into the entranceway, Laura glanced up at her place. Nothing looked any different so she knocked on Jamie's door.

Jamie opened, and like the small ass he was (always having a remark) said, "Food is always better when someone else buys and flies." Laura said nothing and placed the bag on the coffee table.

As they were eating she told him about the feelings of being watched and about the guy she had seen, not what her imagination did, just the guy. She asked him what he thought.

Laughing at her, with a piece of pizza in his mouth, he said, "Damn, Laura. You have a stalker!"

She just squinted her eyes as if to say "fuck you" but said nothing and ate some more. They were both very full. Shoot, they had almost eaten all the pie and salad when Laura said, "Is there anywhere a person can do a family trace or research a family name?"

Jamie said, "Try the library." When she asked what time they opened, he just shrugged his shoulders and replied, "Hell. I don't know. I don't even read."

"Well, okay then. I'm going to bed so I can get up early and see." Laura exited the room, going into the spare bedroom. She closed the door and clothes and all fell into the bed.

"Damn, what a night," she recalled to herself and, without even realizing it, fell fast asleep or so she thought. As the REM sleep started, she was in the house that she had dreamed about that day at the hospital.

This time she was standing outside one of the rooms, the one the shadows were moving in. As she reached out to open the door, she heard a scuffle and a loud scream on the other side. She opened the door forcefully and said, "What the hell?" Looking around she saw no one. "Now I know what I heard. What's going on?" she asked herself. But there was no one other than herself inside the room.

Walking around it, she started to notice things on the dresser and pictures on the walls. The walls and furniture were outdated. Most of the pictures were in black and white. Only a few pictures were in color and the nightstand had a doily on it. "So grandparent style," Laura quietly said to herself. What caught her attention was one of the pictures on the nightstand in the comer. On top was a lamp and under the lamp was what looked like a photo of her and her mom, but she never remembered ever dressing like that or ever taking a black-and-white picture. Walking over to get a better look, she really thought it was a picture of herself. But when she picked it up and looked more closely, she realized it was a picture of her mom and she guessed the older woman (well, she wasn't that old, mid to late twenties) was probably her grandmother.

The only memories that Laura had of her grandmother were from the stories her mother had told of her. She had died many years before Laura was born, but the stories were of how she was a careful and loving person. She always saw the good side of people instead of the bad, but Laura was never told how she died and that's something she had always wondered about.

Still holding the photo and now really looking, she noticed the girl in the frame had on a necklace that looked like the one Laura had on now. In the dream she grabbed the necklace and a wobble came onto her and she felt herself almost fainting. Letting go of the necklace, she dropped the photo at the same time and the dream (or was it a nightmare) ended.

Laura found herself sitting up in bed with a sweaty sheen to her skin and she was breathing really fast. "Holy shit, what's going on?" Laura said, wiping her face with her hands and trying to think about what she had just seen in her head. "That's it! Now I'm going to get to the bottom of all this crap!" She got up and headed into the bathroom. As she wet her face, she looked into the mirror and got that strange feeling of being watched. She looked around the small room to confirm that no one was there, but the feeling persisted. She went back to the bedroom and lay back down on the bed, but although she tried, she couldn't get back to sleep.

Daylight came way too fast today. It really dragged her down since she didn't have much sleep, but she needed to find out what was going on. Reluctantly she got her clothes together and headed toward the shower. She heard the sounds of water running in the bathroom and thought Jamie must be already there so she waited in the hall.

In a very short time the water was off and the door opened. Jamie was standing there in only a towel. "Good morning, roomie. What's happening?" he said in his cheery way.

Laura just growled a "yep" and passed him on the way in. Closing the door she undressed and got into the water.

Now all wet and with her head under the water, she got that feeling again. She lifted her head and poked it through the shower curtain. She thought that maybe Jamie had come in, but the door was still locked!

Damn it, man, she thought. She started to soap up, and as her head was underwater, she felt a pair of hands on her back. This really freaked her out. She said, "What the fuck do you..." She stopped in mid-sentence. Wiping her eyes from the soap, she realized there was no one there but her.

Not realizing she was hanging on to the locket, she heard a voice in her mind. "Your skin is very soft. Would you like me to wash you?"

Freaked out now, Laura didn't think twice about getting out. She just got out!

Barely drying, she rushed from the room and ran smack in to Jamie with an oomph. "Do you have a ghost in your place because someone or something just touched me in the shower?"

Looking at her like she was nuts. He said, "You're nuts!"

"No really," she said.

"You Americans are weird, Laura," he replied. "No, I don't have any ghosts or spooks that I know of. It's probably your imagination from what happened last night with your loft and all."

"Yeah, you're probably right. I'm going to go to the library. Want to go?"

"No," he answered. "I have a tech class today so sorry, but good luck," and he disappeared back into the bathroom.

Back in her bedroom and still nervous, she dressed and put her make-up on. As she grabbed her purse, she knocked on the door to the bathroom. "I'm gone, see you later today."

Jamie said, "Yeah, on the counter is a key I had made for you. Forgot to tell you about it last night."

"Thanks, see ya," she said, walking over to get the key and leaving.

CHAPTER
six

Stopping at the comer and waiting for the bus, Laura kept an eye on everyone around her. With everything that was going on since yesterday, she felt like anyone and everybody was a person of interest. Not knowing why someone would tear her apartment up, she now felt violated.

Hearing the squeak of brakes, Laura got up and stood in line with everyone to get on the bus. The door opened and a hefty, over-weight man was behind the wheel. He was chewing on what Laura thought was gum because he was slightly smacking his lips as he chewed. *Yuck, that's gross*, Laura thought. She climbed the three steps up, paid her money, and took a seat.

Looking out the window and watching all the people going about their daily "do's," she wondered what or even how she was going to stand this family information investigation. "Ding!" the alarm for a bus stop sounded. A couple got off and with a "rummph" the bus continued.

After another "ding" she finally heard the "ding" that indicated her stop, Mulch Street. Standing up and getting into the aisle heading to the doors to get out, she noticed the driver smiled at her. "Have a good day, luv." His smile was wide with brown-colored teeth, a few missing.

She thought to herself, *Thank God I'm not eating because I just might puke,* but she smiled back to him just to be nice. She exited and started to walk the street toward the block to the library, but on the way, she started wondering why she was doing this. *You should just let the past be the past and not meddle in things*, she thought.

That thought was wiped away quickly when she thought of her place being ransacked. What would have happened if she was there at the time?

Laura saw the library. (Who could miss it? It was huge!) She looked onto the brick building with the banners and people all handing out reading, studying, or just gathered to talk, but what really got her attention were the gargoyles she saw at the top of the building.

Some looked like bats and others like the heads of dragons, but the one that really made her uncomfortable was the one that looked like a man. She could have sworn it resembled the guy from the other night, yet this cement face had what looked like fangs in its large mouth.

Oh man, I've really got to grab myself. I'm starting to see things now, she thought as she hopped up the stairs into the inner workings of the building.

Walking through the revolving doors, she saw that there were more people outside than in the building. Surprised, she headed toward the information desk. She stopped in front of a pretty college kid with odd-looking glasses. Laura said, "Excuse me, but I need help looking up my family background."

Smiling, the girl showed an unexpected mouth full of braces. She pointed down the hall and said, "You have to go down to the ancestry room. It's down the hall to the end. Turn left to the stairs, down the stairs to the door that says Ancestry. You want to speak with Mr. Dobbs. I'll let him know you're on your way. What's your name?"

"Laura Wilds, thanks," she replied and headed on her way.

"Okay, that was a left and down the stairs to the door marked … ," she repeated in her head. Soon she was standing right in front of the door and knocked.

"Come in," she heard from the other side. Opening the door she looked around and saw there were papers strewn everywhere. There were books on shelves, but many of them were scattered about like the papers. From behind one of the stacks of books a small-framed older man with balding hair and really thick dark glasses appeared. If she hadn't actually known he was there, he would have scared the shit out of her. "Hello, young lady. You must be Ms. Wilds?" he asked.

"Yes. I am."

"What can I do for you?" he asked with a soft voice.

"I need to research my family line and don't know where to start. A friend told me to come down here. Can you help me?" she asked.

"Well, that's what I do, missy, so let's get started," he said enthusiastically. "First, what's your full name, your mother's and father's as well, and do you know your grandparents' names? It's more helpful if you know both but not necessary."

Looking at him she said, "My name is Laura May Wilds. My mom's name was Elizabeth Anne Wilds. Do you need maiden names too?"

"Yes, yes, I'm sorry I didn't say that. Sorry, luv."

"Well, hers is Lareabee, and I really don't know what my grandparents' were because they all died before I was born," she replied.

"Where did you live before here, miss?" he asked.

"In California."

"Okay, let's start a spreadsheet." Walking over to the table he took out a large sheet of paper almost like a poster board and started making boxes with names and lines that connected them to each other. Then he went to the computer and started to type. Laura just sat and watched.

Click, click, tap, and click and then he sighed. "Ma'am, I can only go back to your grandmother on your mother's side from here in the UK. Most of your information is back in the States and in Ireland."

"Ireland," she said. "What do you mean?"

"Well, although it looks like you do have some family in England, most come from the green mountains of Ireland," he answered.

"How can I find out that information, sir?" she asked.

"The only thing I can say is go back to the States, get what they have, and take a trip. There are probably records there too!"

"Oh great." Laura sighed.

"Here. Take this and there's no charge, luv. I really didn't mean to send you on a duck chase." He smiled again and said, "Good luck!" and disappeared behind the large stack of books and papers again.

"Thanks to you too. I appreciate it. Bye." And she left back down the small hall up the stairs, turned right and out, nodding to the info girl. Then she went outside with the paper the old man had given her.

"This is great. One more flicking thing that doesn't make any sense!" Walking back to the bus stop to take her back to Jamie's place, she started to think, "I have family from Ireland... damn! Why didn't Mom tell me? But then Mom never did talk about her side of the family much and all I know about Dad is he was a soldier and couldn't take raising a kid so he split before I was old enough to know him. At least I got a name to go on!"

"Here's the bus," she heard someone say. Laura got her money out and waited to board in line. Riding back, there were all kinds of stuff going through her head, but she just jested them and rode. She tried not to think of anything else right now. "Ding" is the last thing that caught her attention, and coming out of her daydreams, she thought it was her stop.

"Wait, I'm getting off here," she yelled before the bus driver closed the doors.

"Hurry up, miss. I've got more people to move," he said.

Getting up and exiting the bus, she was thankful to be almost to the loft because the information she had received had her brain spinning.

CHAPTER
seven

Walking up the street she saw Jamie sitting on the steps talking to a cop. Laura automatically started to wonder what was going on, but as she approached, Laura noticed it was the same guy that had helped her the night of the break-in.

Coming up to them she asked, "What's up?" and Jamie asked her to sit down. He said she probably wouldn't believe what Officer Shamble was going to say, so she sat down.

"Mrs. Wilds," the officer began.

Laura interrupted and said, "Call me Laura, please. My mom was Mrs. Wilds, please."

"Okay, Laura, the prints that were lifted from your loft, well, we just don't know what to think about them because…" And he hesitated.

"What?" Laura said.

"Well, they are from someone that has a record from the early 1900s."

Laura just sat on the steps, probably looking really stupid, and said, "How can that be? This is 2009. No one can have prints from a hundred years ago."

"That's what we thought so we ran them again, and they came back with the same answer and everything," said the cop.

"Who is it?" Laura practically shouted.

The officer answered, "I can't tell you that information. It's an open case, but if you want to come down to the precinct and talk to my chief in the morning, he should be able to help."

"You've got to be kidding me," she said. "Sure, I'll come down. Thanks, Officer."

He nodded his hat and turned to his car and left.

"Okay, that's really screwed up. They know but won't tell me! Really, Jamie, this really sucks," Laura lashed out.

Jamie just sat on his cement stair, shaking his head. "That's our public servants for ya. They know nothing and do as little as possible."

"Will you go with me to the station in the morning?" she asked.

Of course having to have a smart thing to say, Jamie said, "As long as you buy I fly, but coffee comes first."

"It's a deal," Laura replied.

"It's getting late and I have a date tonight," Jamie said. So handing Laura the keys to the apartment, he got up and hustled into the double door to get ready, leaving Laura alone on the stoop. Sitting there she let her mind wonder on the "what if's" again. With what she learned at the library and the unknown of the station, she thought, *Can it get any weirder than this?* Grabbing her necklace locket, she had a thought that might have come from her mother, "If you search for answers, the answers you receive might not be what you want."

Still clutching it, she then answered the voice, "Why are you playing with me? What is it that is hidden?" Letting go she was brought out of the dream state that only lasts a snap in time, but now she thought that whatever it was, she was going to get to the bottom of what this craziness was no matter what the end is.

Getting up and going inside she sat down on the sofa and started to channel surf, but there was nothing on the TV except talk shows and those silly English skit shows that she thought were really stupid. Hearing water stop in the shower and Jamie going into her room, she got up to get a beer before putting on one of the DVD movies.

Grabbing a cold one out and with a "psssphth" of the cap, she raised and gulped a good one. As she started to drink, she heard "ahhhh," but the sound came after the swallow so she knew it wasn't her own voice. Jamie was standing there watching her.

"Beer is always good when it's cold," Jamie said.

"Shit, dude, don't do that!" a startled Laura shouted. Noticing how he was dressed she whistled and said in a joking manner (because she already knew the answer), "Who's the girl you're all dressed up for?"

"As you know, girlie girl, she's a he and 'her' name is Trent. I met him last week at the club and 00000 he is $000 fine! Maybe I'll get lucky, so if you hear screaming don't call the cops, okay?"

"Okay, Mr. Whore Bags, I won't," she said as she was walking to the living room to start the movie.

Jamie disappeared back in to his room as Laura lifted her legs onto the coffee table and pushed Play, chugging the beer again. As a honk came from outside she shouted, "Yo, dude, your date is here. Can I meet him? Can I? Can I? Can I?" She jokingly smiled at him.

"No, you may not and wish me luck," he replied on his way out the door.

Getting up after him to lock the door, click, click of the chain lock, she returned to the movie and her beer. "Yes, silence," was the murmur on her lips.

Before she knew it, watching the television and movie had put her to sleep. Soon static was the only thing on when the rapping of the door woke her.

"Let me in. Damn, it's cold out!" she heard from the other side of the door.

Getting up she heard her knees cracking and Laura cursed herself, "Damn, I didn't even get to see the end of the movie. I'm coming. Keep your knickers on!"

Taking a couple of minutes to get all the locks off with being half asleep Laura opened the door to find Jamie standing with his hand and arms all wrapped around himself to keep warm.

"Sorry, I fell asleep watching the movie. Where's what's his face?" she asked.

"He turned out to be a loser lush, all drunk and hitting on everybody. What a jerk. I left him hanging on someone's arm at the bar," said Jamie.

"Did you have some fun tonight?"

"Yeah, until loser Trent got drinks in him, then it was downhill from there," Jamie replied.

"Okay, then. I'm going to be going to bed, g'night," said Laura. She headed to take a piss and then onto the bedroom where she collapsed on the bed.

CHAPTER
eight

The alarm went off and Laura snoozed the button. Fifteen minutes later, "Buzz, buzz, buzz," the alarm said again.

Laura got up yawning and stretching, feeling like she had slept for three days. "Damn, I was tired," she said as she opened the door and knocked on Jamie's. "Dude, are you still going with me?"

"Yeah, can you give me a few minutes to get dressed?" he answered.

Both now dressed and munched out on some dark toast and coffee, then headed to the bus stop.

"You know, when we get there, he still might not tell you anything and we got up for nothing," Jamie said.

"Yeah, but he might and you don't think it's weird with what the cop, what's-his-face said about the fingerprints?" she answered.

"Well, yeah, but—" and he was cut off when the bus pulled into the stop. Laura pulled the fare out for the both of them, told the driver she was paying for two, and he just smiled and waved them on.

Finding a seat together at this time of the morning was not easy so they climbed the stairs to the upper seating level. Luckily, they found two seats way in the back. Neither of them said much on the ride down. They just watched the many differences in people coming and going.

The ride wasn't very long, but it had a lot of stops so it felt like it lasted forever. Then the ding of their stop finally sounded.

Seeing the street sign of ( ) and ( ), they got up, walked back down and out, said "thank you" to the driver who just smiled, and hopped off.

Standing as the bus rode off Laura asked Jamie again if he was ready and again it was a short reply of "Yep, let's go."

The station wasn't far from the stop, and climbing the stairs, Laura said jokingly, "Do all the buildings in this town have stairs? It kinda seems like it."

"Hell, if I know," Jamie said with one of his famous one-liners.

Opening the door to the precinct no. 29, they entered, walked up to the front desk, and asked if the chief was available. The lady asked politely, "Who is calling for him and what is this concerning?"

Laura started to tell her about her place being broken into and the prints and the officer stopping by and ... The lady stopped her and told them to have a seat. She would see if he was in.

Sitting down and watching the commotion in the station, a heavyset man dressed in the police blues and holding a couple of folders in his hand approached them.

"Mr. and Mrs. Wilds?" the man asked. "Good morning. My name is Chief Stubbnicke."

Laura looked up and said, "Ms. Wilds and this is my friend Jamie Collins and we aren't married."

"Oh, I'm so very sorry. Do you or can you answer some questions that I have? If you could, you might be able to help to our investigation. The answers might help the both of us. Please follow me to my office."

Jamie looked at Laura and gave her one of his silly "let's do it" looks with his shit-eating grin and followed the chief. As the chief entered his office, he asked them to have a seat and closed the door. He sat down in his cushy, well-worn chair and placed his hands on his desk. "Ms. Wilds, do you know anyone who would want anything from you or thinks that you might even have something maybe you don't even know you have?"

"No, sir, I don't. The only things I brought with me from the States were my clothes and what few things my mom had and that wasn't much. Just photos, books, and papers that she had forever from my grandmother," Laura told him.

"Have you looked at these things closely?" the chief asked.

"Well, no. They are just stuff that's in a box my mom, well, she always kept them so I guessed they were important to her and I kept them too. Why? Do you think there's something in those? I will look if you want me to."

"If you could," he answered, "and see if something strange stands out at you. Now, Ms. Wilds, this is going to sound far-fetched—I can't even believe it myself—but we have these prints that were taken from your home. Ah, I really don't know how to say this, but to say it, they are…Damn it. It doesn't make any sense because they are over a hundred years old! Now, I know as you do that no one can live that long, and if they do, I want some of that they are taking," the chief replied in a joking manner.

Laura and Jamie just looked at him and Laura asked, "So what does this mean? I have a really, really old person stalking me or someone is playing a bad joke? Whatever it is my place has been torn to bits and oh, yeah—can I go into it now? I would really like to sleep on my own bed."

Placing his hands over his face Chief Stubbnickle said, "Yes, I don't see why you can't. Just please look into those papers for us and call me directly if you find anything that seems even slightly out of place."

Handing her his card and giving another to Jamie, he politely said, "Thank you for coming down and stay in touch."

Opening the door and getting a handshake on the way out, both Laura and Jamie said at the same time, "Nothing we didn't already know." Laura added, "Yeah, but will you help me with the papers from my mom?"

Jamie just looked at her and said, "You might want to do that by yourself. It's your family and all."

Agreeing, she said, "Yep, you're right. I didn't think."

"Cool and all righty. Since you're buying, I am starved," Jamie said as he rubbed his belly with his hand.

"Breakfast or lunch?" Laura asked.

"Both, you know me ... Bottomless."

Walking down toward the bus stop the smell of coffee wisped past their noses with the faintest following scent of cherries and apples.

Jamie spoke up, "Let's eat."

"Great, I really need some coffee," Laura said.

Crossing the street quickly so as not to get run over and winding around people, chairs, and tables that sat outside stores, they found where the mouth-watering smell came from. Hurrying in and getting into line, Jamie put his order in with Laura, then went to grab a seat outside.

Giving their request and sliding down to pay and wait, Laura couldn't help but to silently think about what was in those papers because she had never really looked at them, even when her mother was alive. Hell, she couldn't remember really seeing her mom look at them either.

"Ma'am, your order's done," a teenage boy with braces said, startling her back to reality.

"Oh, what? Sorry, thanks." She smiled as she headed outside.

"Here you go, Pig Man," she said to Jamie and giggled.

"Thank you and you'll be getting your tip later." He also giggled back sarcastically.

Sitting there each of them didn't really say much. They just ate and, when done, cleaned off the table and threw the trash away. They started for the bus stop, not talking even at the bus stop or even on the ride back.

They heard the familiar ding of the bus sounding and Jamie said, "This is our stop." As they got off Laura asked him again if he was sure he really didn't want to help.

"Nope, if you find something or get stuck you know where I'll be, at home in bed."

"Sure, thanks," she said, and reaching into her pocket to get her keys out, Laura started climbing the staircase and Jamie went into his apartment, leaving her alone. Getting to the top she just stood looking at the door. "Fuck, get your scaredy candy ass in there. Ain't no one there," she told herself.

CHAPTER
nine

Pushing the key and turning to hear the deadbolt click, then pushing open the door, she walked in. Laura turned around and relocked the door and went into the living room.

"God, what a mess!" Laura said. "Where do I start?"

Grabbing onto the chair that was upside down and making it right up she said, "This is garbage and the other sofa too."

Now after a good while of straightening, piling, and rearranging the place, it started looking like her place again, only with a big trash pile near the wall. "This room is done. Now onto the kitchen." But when she stood there looking at the open cupboards, glasses, plates, and everything else all over, Laura just shook her head and thought, *Later.*

She went into her untouched bedroom as the feeling of wonder came upon her. Why was the rest of the house thrown around but not this room? "Crazy" was the only word that came to mind. She sat on the bed and was soon lying on the bed and was asleep before even realizing it. She woke up and looked around because, for a split second, she didn't remember or maybe forgot due to sleep where she was. She glanced at the window, which showed the time of day being late. She thought, *Shit, what time is it?* Then she looked at the clock on the dresser that read 9:27 p.m.

Wow, I must have been really tired, but sleeping in my own bed again was wonderful, she thought as she sat up. *Now where's that box with Mom's papers in it?*

Walking over to the closet and pulling some shoes and stuff out there it was in the comer tucked away. As she grabbed it and lifted it onto the bed, she blew the dust off the cover, reminding herself of a sandstorm in Cali. Laura opened it slowly, hoping no lid bugs or spiders were going to jump out at her. Placing the lid on the floor and sitting down, she reached in and grabbed a handful of photos and papers. She organized them as to category—papers in one pile, pictures in another, and things she didn't know what they were in another. Everything was really boring until she found an old picture of her grandma standing with a younger-looking guy who had his arm around her as if they were a couple or something. But that's not what caught Laura's attention. What caught her attention was the guy looked like the very same one she had seen under the light post a few nights ago.

No way! That can't be him, she thought.

Still looking at it while she placed the photo up into a new pile on the pillow, she grabbed more from the box, still mostly just junk, but some or most were deeds and ownership papers of places she had never seen or let alone heard of. Laura put them with the photo on her pillow to continue with another handful, only this grab pulled out letters all bundled into a stack and tied with a pretty pink string.

All of them were letters to her grandma and some could still be read with addresses and names of from and to. Laura untied the string and, opening the first one, pulled out the paper that was folded in half and unfolded it very carefully and looked at the writing. It was very old type, like scripted but hand done and really pretty, Laura thought. As she read, it started:

To My Beloved,

Although many days and years have passed with us, I still think of you as the beautiful young woman I met. Even as you grow older and your body does also and mine...

Then the letter becomes unreadable but the date was still there at the top: February 14, 1946.

Looking at the date on the letter, Laura started to silently do the math. If this was to Grandma, then she was still young when this letter was written. *I wonder if Mom knew any of this,* Laura thought. Tossing the first onto the pillow and fingering down to one half way, she pulled another one out. Again it was addressed to her grandma, so she took the paper out and unfolded this one. She found it had a smoothed flower inside, with only these words written,

"Our Love, Curtis M."

"Now who the hell is Curtis M. and what's he doing messing around with Grandma?" Questions onto questions and the more Laura tried to figure this out the deeper in secrecy it got. Now really wanting to know what was going on, she started taking all the letters out of their envelopes and reached over to the night stand and opened one of the drawers to pull out the box of paper clips she sometimes used for stuff. Carefully placing one on each letter with its original envelope, Laura began to put them in order chronologically.

"By the looks of this stack, I will be here for a while," she said to herself. She glanced at the clock, which now read 11:12 p.m. "Coffee is what I'm going to need." Carefully getting up so as not to have any of the papers fall, she went into the kitchen.

Returning with a steaming mug full and placing it on the night stand next to the clock, she carefully hopped on to the bed and started to read and clip.

Most of the letters she could read, but some of them had long ago dried wet spots that had smeared the ink. Maybe it was the teardrops of the person who had read them. Smears unreadable or readable, Laura put them into the pile, sorting as she went until she found one she opened that had instead of her grandmother's name, Elizabeth Wilds. Seeing this Laura just about choked on the coffee she had just swallowed. Aloud she said, "Shit, no way!"

Re-examining the envelope more carefully to see if her mom had just thrown it in as an old keepsake, Laura read the return name and address. It had a name, no house number, and the name put a cold chill right up her spine. It was the very same name as her grandmother's letters—Curtis M. The last name was still only an "M." Now she wanted to know what was going on.

CHAPTER

ten

Remembering that she had promised her friend Julie to meet her at the coffee shop at eleven and seeing the clock, which now was past midnight, she put everything back into the box. This time they were sorted to be picked through later. She took her clothes off, tossing them into a heap on the floor, and crawled into bed, reaching to see the alarm for 9:15 a.m. She shut the lamp off and lay down.

Sleep was not what she got this night because, soon after closing her eyes and drifting off, the most realistic dream grabbed her.

It was her on top of a large coastal rise of a cliff, overlooking the sea shore in a place she had never been. She was lying on top of a blanket that felt as if it was made out of the softest material ever sewed together. Looking down at herself she saw that she was wearing a half-length green emerald dress almost the same color as the waters below, and in her hand was a glass of red liquid that she thought was wine.

What was really shocking in this dream was the pair of legs, strong and long that ran down the length of her as if she was sitting between them, leaning onto someone's chest. She was leaning her head back and the man that sat behind her looked just like the man under the lamp post. He was rubbing her shoulders with his strong, long-fingered hands, and yet when this should have frightened her, it didn't. She was contented and had the strange feeling of being safe within this hold.

Still looking up at this man's face, Laura asked, "Who are you?"

He just slanted his head down to look her in the eyes and she thought, *What eyes he had! Oh, those eyes.* They were like the coolest color of a calm ocean. So blue a person could lose themselves looking into them.

And then he spoke. "Yours are not so bad to look at either, my dearest Laura. You may call me Curtis. I am Curtis McCordly, of the Highlands McCordleys." Then he took his left hand off her left shoulder and placed it under her chin, lifting it up just a bit, and as he did this, he tilted his head and placed his lips upon hers, giving her the softest and most passionate kiss a man could or has ever given her.

Laura melted when he did this, and then his right hand slid down to just under her right breast. As he caressed it, his thumb brushed over her nipple, which was now very hard and very sensitive to his touch. As he rubbed her breast, a tightness began to start at the lower part of her belly and a moistness began between her legs.

Lifting his head as if giving her a moment to breathe, he spoke very softly and directly at her. "I have waited many years for you, Laura Wilds."

This was when the dream became reality as the beeping of the alarm drew her back to her bed and her bedroom.

As the alarm beeped, she woke up in a daze of shock and dismay to find the covers crumbled around her body. Her body was alive as if the dream was actually real.

"Holy shit, that was wacked. I really need to get out more." Then unraveling the covers she found that down there between her legs she was wet, as if she had a wet dream.

"You're kidding me," Laura said out loud.

Seeing this and remembering her dream, she got up and went to the shower. It took little time to turn the water on and get into the shower since she already had no clothes on. When she was under the warm spray of the water, her mind wandered back to the dream and him, Curtis McCordly. As she thought about it and him, she finished what had started in that dream herself.

When the muscles of her body tightened around her finger and her own juices dripped into her hand, she thought that her legs were going to drop off right there in the shower. Finishing with one last moan and pulling her finger out, Laura felt as if she had died and gone to heaven. It had been that long.

Opening her eyes and feeling a serene calmness come over her, she washed her hair and body with soap. She got out to see if she was going to be late for her coffee date.

She picked her clothes off the floor and threw them into the hamper. She opened the closet and pulled out a clean pair of jeans and a T-shirt. She walked over to the dresser and opened the tiny drawer on the left for a pair of panties and a bra and got dressed.

Still feeling the "ahhh" of the shower, she thought, with a smile, *I'm going to keep that to myself.*

Heading out the door she almost forgot to turn off the light from last night. She turned around and walked into the still-messy room. She pushed the button on the coffeemaker and pulled the plug, something her mom always did, and she just did it too.

Mom always said, "If it ain't plugged in, it can't start a fire." She was right, as moms usually are, closing the door as she walked out and locking all three of the locks.

Like it really helped the last time, she thought. But she did it anyway out of habit and headed out for some coffee and a good talk or maybe some juicy gossip with "Jules" as Laura called her.

CHAPTER
eleven

The coffee shop was only a couple of blocks away so there was no need to catch the bus. Walking casually her mind couldn't stop rewinding and thinking about that dream and the mysterious Curtis who knew her name—how? A lot of questions began to emerge as these blocks soon felt like miles. *Who is he? Where is he? Why is—or hell—what year is he from?*

She stopped the "W" thinking short. That's the weird part because if the prints were from way back when and now the letters were from way back when, then Laura's imagination went nuts: ghost, werewolf, maybe even a vampire. "No way," she said out loud, and when she did, a lady with a large grocery bag and a purse on her arm walked by looking at Laura as if she was a madwoman or something. Laura just smiled and said "good day," embarrassed to hell.

Rounding the corner and seeing Jules sitting outside already eating and drinking, Laura waved, with Jules waving back. Getting to the table, Jules looked at her clock on her cell phone and smiled as she said, "You're late."

"Yeah, I know. Sorry."

"Late night? With who?" Jules asked.

Laura just smiled and said, "No one," as if she'd believe her anyway. She said that she was just going through some boxes of her mom's and straightening out after the break-in.

"What break-in? You didn't call me. Are you okay? Did they take anything? And why the hell didn't you call me?" Jules said, almost scolding as she did.

"One," Laura started, "yes, I am okay and no nothing was taken, just broken up, and it was very late, and shit, Jamie was downstairs so I just stayed with him. I didn't call you because you would've insisted I stay at your place with you and Roger and I didn't want to intrude."

"Okay then, but what happened?"

So Laura told her she called the cops, made a report, and then started to tell her about the fingerprints but stopped, and said that the case was just being opened as a burglary instead.

"Well, as long as you're okay, I'm okay too, but if you need me, you'd better call me, okay?" Julie replied. Then she said, with a shit-eating grin, "Are you ready to hear something?"

"What?" said Laura.

"Roger asked me to marry him!" she replied.

"Oh, no way! That's too pretty, and oh, so cool, Jules," Laura said and stood up and bent over to hug her only female friend in London.

Now excited and thankful not to be thinking about the last couple of days, Laura asked with excitement in her voice, "When is it and I am going to be a bridesmaid, right? Oh, and what color of dresses do we get to wear?"

Julie sighed and said kind of sadly, "The date isn't set yet, because we don't know when or if Roger's going to get shipped out yet. We will know by the end of the week and today is—"

"He at least asked. You're right, I'm sorry again. I just got excited because I know you've been wanting this day for a long time, since little Bree was born six months ago."

"I know and now it's here. I still or we still have to wait. This really sucks cucumbers," Julie said.

"Well, let's go shopping. My treat for this special day. I want to get you something new," Laura requested as she sipped out of Jules's coffee. "Hold on. Let me leave a tip." She reached into her pocketbook for some change. "I got it, Jules," said Laura as she sprung a buck out of her jeans.

"Let's go," they both said at the same time with a giggle and started to walk arm in arm.

In this part of town, a lot of the shops were along the streets just as they had been for many years. What a lot of people don't know about London is that, in many areas, the people have kept the traditions of wholesome life. Although the merchandise changes, the family names stay the same.

The first shop was a clothing boutique. When the two walked in, they knew all this was going to be was window-shopping.

Jules was soon going to grow out of everything she has now and Laura, already not being able to wear anything, it was an in-and-out process, but they were polite when the clerk asked if she could help with anything.

"No, thanks, we're just looking," they answered.

Within moments Julie and Laura exited the shop and were walking down the stone pathway up to another shop.

This time it was a bookstore and Jules said to Laura, "We need to go in here. I want to get some baby books."

Laura answered with a large and happy smile, "Okie-dokie."

As they entered, a cow bell above the door gave out a large "clunky clang" and again as the door closed. The smell of the store when entering was old, musty with a light aerosol scent but one knew it was a bookstore because from everywhere one could see there were books of all sizes, shapes, colors, etc. There were books on shelves, above shelves, and even stacked upon the floor.

Laura looked at Jules, and placing her two fingers over her nose from the smell, she said, "Do you think they sell any of these or just horde them?"

The two quickly laughed between when just behind them a very low sound of clearing a person's throat was heard. They both turned to see an older lady no more than four foot nothing and dressed as if she was straight from the books that surrounded her. Her age looked to be the same except for her eyes.

Laura looked at her and had the strangest feeling that this woman could see straight through her or knew more than she would ever say.

Jules, being Jules, asked the woman, "Really, does this store have anything that anyone under fifty years old would read?"

Laura couldn't believe her ears as she heard what her friend said and cut her off very sternly, "What she means is...are there any up-to-date books?"

Looking at Jules's face with a look that said that was uncalled for, the old woman started to speak as if she ignored what Jules had just said and looked directly at Laura. "What are you seeking, answers or questions?"

In Laura's mind, her first thought was "answers" because of the present happenings, but she didn't say that. Instead she asked about books on Ireland and especially any homes with or about the clans and names of the lands, also any baby or new mothers' book.

"I have many books on lands far away, but what you are seeking will be in the back over near a large chest of drawers on the left." Then with a sigh that almost sounded like the woman was going to die right there, she reached out and took Laura's arm, and at the second this connection happened, the old woman spoke. "This is a better day today than yesterday and tomorrow to see the rising sun."

Letting go quickly and already shocking Laura, the woman gestured for her to follow. Jules, who was not quick near enough to hear what was just said, was still close enough to say, "I am heading back here. I'll be right back." She just nodded without looking up as she was looking at a book.

The old woman and Laura headed back to the back of the store through what Laura thought was a labyrinth of books. They went to the very ends of the rows near the chest just as she had said and then stopped, bending down to one of the bottom shelves.

The old woman picked out a book and slowly rose from the position she was in. She said, "I'm not young anymore. These old bones don't let me do anymore what they used to." She smiled. "Now I think this is what you're looking for, dearie, but may I ask you a question without you getting ruffled?"

"Sure," Laura replied.

"Are you sure you are ready to seek the answers that you might find? When I touched your arm, your colors were of darkness and sadness."

Now really looking at this strange old woman, Laura asked her, "What do you know of that with just a touch and what am I going to do?" The question was more of a snapping demand and in an untrusting way but the old woman didn't falter.

She just stood there and said, "I am a very old lady who has seen many things in my days and traveled just as far but with a curse my grandmother once spoke of. Now with each year ending, understand the decisions we make today are not always the right ones and you have many to reach for."

Not really understanding, Laura just quickly asked her how much for the books because she wanted to leave right now.

The woman just said, "It is yours. No charge as you will be using it more than this old shelf, but a donation would be just."

Reaching into her purse, Laura brought out a ten dollar US paper money and said "thank you" as she walked away to the front.

Seeing Julie still thumbing through dusty books she yelled out, "I'm done. Let's go."

Jules placed the book she had down anywhere, saying, "Cool," and they left with the cow bell again announcing their exit.

"What happened back there? You act as if you just got the shit scared out of you," Jules said.

"She was a really weird woman. She was saying things that made no sense, and then she told me that I could have this book. That I would be needing it," Laura told her.

"Yeah, that is strange and spooky, and really so was that place. Let's eat. I'm starving!" Jules said. "I'm eating for two now."

Laura just smiled and smacked her lips as if to say yes. After getting a quick snack and seeing that it was getting on in the day, Julie said, "I have to get home and cook some dinner. Rog likes to eat after work at a normal time."

So the two of them hugged and promised another day of shopping sometime in the near future, hopefully, without any old bookstore in it and they parted ways.

Again walking alone, Laura's mind recalled what the old woman had spoken about. *I wonder what she meant about the "decisions we make" thing. Mmmm. Wonder if she could tell me anything more.* Laura began to walk back to the store.

Walking up to the door and grabbing the handle, she found that it was locked and, stepping back, saw a closed sign in the front window, saying to herself, "This is strange. We were just here an hour ago."

She went to the store next to it and asked the clerk behind the counter, "Do you know when they open the bookstore next door? We were just in there and now it's closed."

The clerk looked at her with a funny expression and said, "You weren't in that store, ma'am. It's been closed up tight since old Mrs. Ferison died three months ago."

Now wide eyed, Laura couldn't believe her ears. "No, really, I was just in there and a little old lady was in there, no bigger than this." She showed her height with her hand to the clerk.

"Ma'am, I'm telling you no one has even opened those doors for three months. You must be thinking of another shop!"

"Fine, thanks," Laura snapped back and left. "Okay, my life has really got to stop getting any weirder! Mom, what the hell is going on? What did you and grandma have or what were you doing?" Laura spoke out loud thinking she was going nuts. The walk home was muddled with all sorts of thoughts in her mind.

Holding the book in one hand and reaching for her necklace she instantly thought of the seashore and him. The thought brought a smile. *All this must be a dream and I am going to wake up soon*, was the lingering works of her mind as she rounded the corner to her place.

She got to the stairs and looked up—nope, no lights on. That's a good sign, so she walked through the entrance into the hall and just about went to see Jamie but stopped because she knew he would be sleeping. *He's always sleeping*, she thought, with a smile on her face so she trounced up the stairs to her door.

She unlocked the three locks and went in, not forgetting to relock them. She started dropping things and stripping off as she walked into the living room. She turned on the telly, finding nothing but re-runs and news.

Turning on the light and seeing the box right where she left it, she went into the bathroom and started the water for a shower. She began to undress, but just when she was almost naked, she realized she forgot the book. Wearing nothing but a bra, she went back to the table where she left it open when she got home.

Now throwing it onto the bed and seeing it flop as it hit her comforter she went back into the bathroom, taking the last thing off, her bra, as she got under the water.

Closing her eyes as the water relaxed her, she couldn't help but think of this morning. Slowly she placed the soap on her wet chest and began to lather herself up, coming from her chest to arms and then to her feet and legs, but it just wasn't the same, and feeling almost disgruntled, she rinsed and got out to dry off.

Not really wanting to get dress for bed yet, she just sat down on her bed, grabbing the book and fluffing the pillows so she could sit up and open it.

When she did, the smell of "old" rose in to her nose and she let out a "whew" but it faded fast and she turned the page that read "Clans of the Highlands" and dates from it said 1644 to 1979.

Wow, that's a lot of years, she thought and turned the page.

There was a beautiful drawing of a village with IDs, dogs, people, and even crops in the background with a large castle looking home up on the hill looking down over the picture. *Oh, how pretty*, she thought. *It would make a great picture on someone's wall.*

Then turning again and it was a family tree with lots of people's names in each block that attached to other blocks or squares. Reading from top to bottom and having to turn the whole book lengthwise to read it, the first name said, "Isaac Van Bothen *VanBothen Clan 1644–1677," and so on...

FLUTTER OF A BROKEN HEART

Van Bothen Clan
1614–1656

Isaac Van Bothen

McNermie Clan 1677

↓

Cresta Van Bothen | Borus McNermie

↓

Twins

Louie Calroy (M. 1669) — Vandilyn McMemie (fire destroyed home)
B. 1649–D. 1701   B. 1653–D. 1701
                    Victor McMemie (died at birth)

Elizabeth Calroy ——— Dan Calroy ——— Mella Calroy (baby 1671)
B. 1669–D. 1701   B. 1670–D. 1673   D. in 1695

↓

Danthony Cordly (M. 1685)   Cordly Clan 1685
B. 1656–D. 1700

↓

Cyril Cordly   Jytel Cordly (M.1708) — Joycline Lemire
B. 1686–D. 1687   B. 1687–D. 1733   B. 1688–D.

↓

Twins

Brandywine Cordly   Brogus Cordly (M.1716) — Ann McGregor
B. 1704–D. 1710   B. 1704–D. 1731

Twins

Stephano Cordly   Stephany Cordly
B. 1722   B. 1722

Curtus Cordly (M. 1748) — Yseif Islings ——— Destiny Cordly
B. 1730–1755   B. 1733–D. 1758   B. 1729–1740

↓

Curtis Cordly II–B. 1749–

As she read the chart and went to the bottom of the page, it turned a dark wet color and the rest was unreadable due age, dampness, or who knew what. But here was his name or one of his relations, not once but twice. Sitting there she thought, *At least I am not totally insane, because there was a Curtis Cordley. But how could anyone live now to have fingerprints and how, well*... Her mind just couldn't think like that. *It's impossible.*

Looking at the clock it was way past sleeping hour for her again, and putting the book on the night stand, she flung the now-dry towel onto the chair next to the bed, scooted her butt up to get under the covers, and turned out the light.

The room was instantly dark. Laying there she thought about what she had just read and the strange day as her eyes became heavy and she drifted into the blackness behind her eyelids.

CHAPTER
twelve

The dark didn't last long because a voice, his voice, was in her left ear as if he was lying right beside her and softly speaking. "Laura, why look into books for answers when I can tell them to you if you shall only ask."

As she heard this, she felt as if someone was moving her hair away from her face.

Laura opened her eyes and there on the left side, lying in her bed, was the dream she knew as Curtis and he was placing her hair out of her face and laying it with one finger around her ear as he spoke. Then with the same finger he drew a line around her jaw and placed his thumb ever so lightly upon her lips and traced them.

She asked him in a hushed voice, "How can you be real? The book says all your family is dead and gone many years ago and how…"

A finger placed over her lips stopped her from speaking any more words and he leaned over and placed a kiss on her cheek while saying, "They are, but I am here now, am I not?" And moving his mouth over to hers he placed a kiss on her lips that made fireworks go off behind her now-closed eyes.

"Mmmun" was the sound coming from her throat and the feeling of his edge calloused hand on the skin of her right breast. Laura lifted her chest into it, welcoming the touch.

Then she rolled over onto her left side and pulled her arms up. One over his small and muscular waist and the other above her head so she could run her fingers through his soft, long, black hair when he said, "Wait. This cannot be done with linens on." And he turned to stand. The room was still and dark as night, but she could see shadows and he was there standing in front of her and taking off what she thought was sweatpants and a T-shirt.

With a giggle she said, "You're wearing sweats and a tee?"

And he said as he was getting back into bed to the same position they were in, "Of course, it is the twenty-first century. I would look quite strange in my homeland attire." He kissed her before she could say another word.

Now he was gently rubbing her body as his lips were putting her into another realm of delight.

He rubbed her body from back to front and back again. Each touch felt as if she would explode. Then he grabbed her butt cheek on the right side and, with a pull, pulled her close to him and she could feel his hardness lying between them, the length of it almost touching the bottom of her breasts. His fingers rounded the bottom of her ass and parted her cheeks from behind. She could feel his long finger playing with the folds of her womanhood.

Then the finger came away and his knee thrust hers up into the air. "Now we can do much better," he said in a heavy breath. His hand was now on the inside of her left thigh and working its way back to where his finger was just moments ago.

Laura took her arm off his waist. She was searching for his length that was between them, and she found it where it laid. Placing her fingers around this, her fingertips could not touch from around. She started to stroke, holding her fingers lightly but snuggly as she went from top to bottom.

Curtis moaned when she started caressing his manhood and with one solid movement impaled his finger into her. Laura squirmed and in a breath spoke a passionate "Oh, more!" as she made her movements the same as his.

Laying there for the longest time, they were both becoming very aware of what was going to happen, and soon, Curtis pushed Laura onto her back and, with the finesse of a master, rolled up onto her, widening her legs as he did.

Placing both his hands onto her hips, he held her and, in one stride, one push, entered her with the moan of a man in ecstasy as she did the same laying beneath him.

Then he was thrusting in and almost completely out of her and back in again. He bent down, kissed her, and said, "Laura Wilds, does thy want to be with me forever?"

In this moment of heated passion she sighed, "Yes, oh, yes!"

He moved his mouth from hers and onto her neck as if to kiss her throat but, instead, as a hard and sudden thrust, went into her with such a force that she was off and he was biting into her neck.

The feeling she was in, she never felt the teeth enter or him sucking her life's fluid from her. She only felt him in her, around her, and the whole world as she knew it had stopped in a single thrust.

She felt her muscles holding and releasing inside as he was swallowing her warm, sweet-tasting blood.

As Curtis felt her body relax and the last love hug from the inside of her thighs release him, he cautiously released his hold on her neck, with a final lick of his tongue over the two little holes where the fangs were, and the wounds were closed.

Lying there in each other's arms, Laura thought she was in heaven when Curtis said, "You are so much more passionate than your grandmother and mother."

Sitting straight up and scrambling off the bed, she couldn't believe what he had said, let alone heard and grabbing onto both sides of her head with both hands she said in an almost scream, "What the hell are you talking about? What are we doing? You're not real. You're in my head! Get out before I start to think I am mad!"

Turning quickly she reached out and pushed the light button on. Looking at the bed with its crumpled sheets and wet stains there was no one but herself in the room. "Oh my God, what is going on? I really am going nuts."

Shaking now and not knowing which way to turn let alone someone to call because they would think she really had gone bonkers, she grabbed her robe and went into the living room to sit and think or "stew" on what had just happened in her bedroom. Turning on the television and really not watching it, her mind drifted only slightly before she shook the thought away with a "no" in her mind.

She grabbed a magazine and thumbed through it when she came across an ad for a fortune teller and stopped to read it. The ad said, "Madame Valerie. Hear your past, present, and future loved ones and love ones to be … 1-888-733-6673 (1-800-SEE-MORE) to make an appointment. Twenty-four hours a day. Seven days a week."

Laura though, *Why not? It couldn't get any worse.* And she picked up the phone and dialed.

The ringer rang about four times and a woman answered, "Good evening, Madame Valerie. Can I help you with your life?"

A silence and Madame Valerie said, "Is anyone there?"

"Yes, I am here. I just don't know what to say," Laura said to her.

"Well, we can start with an appointment if you'd like and go from there," Madame Valerie responded.

Laura hesitated and said, "Can you see me tomorrow or, I mean, today?" She glanced at the clock on the wall.

"Hold on, I'll check." Laura could hear the sound of the receiver being laid down and papers being moved. "Can you come at 11:30 a.m.?"

"Okay, give me directions." Writing down on an envelope that was laying on the coffee table, Laura sat back against the sofa and then let out a chuckle that surprised her because the thought of being crazy was still in her mind. But the feeling between her legs and on her body told her another thing. It was so real.

Hurrying now to get her pants on and wash, she came out being the only person up, making her feel the center of attraction. Blushing, she sat down and waited.

thirteen

Dozing off, Laura was startled awake only a few hours later by the rapping of a knock on the door. "Let me in," the voice said. It was Jamie.

"Hold on." She got up and unlocked the door. Opening it up, she saw a look on his face and said, "What's wrong? You look like shit."

"Thank God it's not you," he said. "You haven't heard what happened early this morning?"

"No. What?"

"They found a body just five blocks from here and it was a female. The description sounded like it was you, so I came straight from the club to make sure it wasn't," Jamie exclaimed.

"I've been home all night. What happened to her?" Laura asked sharply, trying to calm him down.

"Well, that's the weird part. A cop friend of a friend came in after his shift and was telling how they got a call about a woman lying in the park dead. But here is the strange part," he said. "She had all her blood drained out of her and..." He stopped.

"What?" asked Laura.

"And she had two puncture wounds on her neck." Jamie took a big breath to continue. "The friend said it looked like a vampire bite right on her neck."

Lifting her arm to her neck, Laura remembered the dream and the feeling of what Curtis was doing.

"No way, you're joking. This isn't funny," she said sternly.

"No, Laura. I'm not kidding. It just happened maybe three hours ago. But what scared me was the description of the girl and it sounded just like you. With your loft being broken into and the craziness with it, I got scared. So I came over to see if you were okay or if it was…" Jamie stopped there, knowing Laura was okay.

"Jamie, I am okay. I haven't gone anywhere all night, but are you okay because, damn, you look like hell just ran over you twice."

"Well, what do you think someone should look like when they think someone they know might have been just murdered?" he asked.

Laura didn't have an answer. Jamie stood up and with a wink said he was going to go downstairs and get some sleep. He'd been partying all night and this killed his buzz.

"Sorry to be a buzz-kill, but thanks for worrying about me," she said as she walked him to the door.

"Somebody needs to," he said as he started down the stairs back to his place.

Closing and locking the door, Laura said, "He's so gay, but cool."

Then she started into the kitchen to make some coffee because the fortune teller was across town and she would have to take three to four busses to get there.

Pushing the bottom of the coffee maker and heading into the bedroom, she stopped short, looking again at the bed and remembering what Jamie said.

She ran into the bathroom and looked at her neck. Turning into the mirror so she could see herself clearly, pulling the skin tight, she about fainted. Right there, faintly, were two red marks that looked like bug bites but could…?

"Oh, fuck me," Laura said to herself as she was looking at herself in the mirror. Then there was a silent "that's what he did" brushed against her brain as if her brain was talking back to her.

Still holding her neck and thinking the worst, Laura didn't know what to do. She was thinking all kinds of really farfetched and stupid things. Almost a panic was setting in until she stopped herself and again spoke to her brain, "Okay, let's not start really doing the cuckoo thing. It's bad enough you're going to see a fortune teller! God. Mom, what is going on?" That was the last thing that crossed her mind before getting into the shower to get ready for her appointment.

Getting out of the shower and drying off, she still touched her neck and, with a shiver up her spine, remembered the night, the night of such passion she had never had before. Walking into the room and getting into dresser drawers for her clothes, she stopped just for a second and glanced onto the bed as she held a frilly red pair of panties in her hand, wondering if he would like them. Coming back to her senses after a brain talk of "He's only a dream," she grabbed a pair of plain cotton whites and began to dress.

Putting everything on, she went into the kitchen, made herself a cup of coffee, and headed back into the bathroom to put her face on. While there doing her eyes, cheeks, and lips she kept looking at her neck and where the two marks were, taking a fingertip of cover-up and applying it to them, even though no one really could see them, but she rubbed it in until she thought she was covered.

Finishing and sipping on her coffee, which was still very hot, she grabbed up her rings and loose change from the night before and headed out.

Right as she was getting ready to unlock the door, she remembered the book on the nightstand and rushed back to retrieve it. Then out the door she was. Having to get to the bus stop so early in the morning was a drag because of all the people who rode these buses instead of driving.

Getting to the corner at the end of the block, there was already at least twenty people waiting. "Ugh," Laura said to herself.

Now waiting for who knows how long, she got right into queue with everyone else, standing, talking, sipping all different smells of coffee, and of course, shivering because London in the morning is not the warmest place to be.

Someone from the crowd yelled out, "The bus is coming," and everyone started to push and shove to get the best seats upon entering. Stepping up the stairs and seeing a seat midway, she walked to it and sat down next to the elderly woman there before her.

"Morning, miss, where are you traveling to today?" the old lady asked.

Laura smiled and really didn't want to say where exactly but instead just returned with "I have an appointment, and you?"

The old woman started to tell her about how she didn't get her check this month and how that has made her rent late and so on and so on. Laura almost regretted the seat she had chosen, but remembering that her mom always said "There is someone out there less fortunate than you and some don't have anybody to talk to except when traveling to and fro," Laura let the woman talk until a ding was heard and she stood up barely and exited the bus.

As in all travels by bus someone leaves and someone else gets on so the next person to sit next to Laura was a heavyset man, and she moved to the window seat to give him room. Honestly, she didn't want him rubbing any of his fat against her.

The bus moved on and another ding, which was her first transfer stop so she squeezed through the area of the large man and the seat. She got off and waited for the next bus to take her farther on to her destination. The wait was not long so the time frame that she had given herself was still good if the buses ran as they were doing.

Another bus, another round of people, she kept thinking to herself. "Ding" was the sound again and off to another then another. When it was finally the last stop, Laura exited, book in hand and the envelope with the house number and directions on top. Reading it so she could start reading house numbers, she started to walk, glancing up homes and then to paper and back.

The walk was about two blocks but it wasn't bad. Then finally she came to the front steps of Madame Valerie's home (like she could miss it).

CHAPTER

fourteen

The window has a large palm sign with her name above and on the door there was another sign with the moon and stars, which Laura thought was really pretty as she walked up the stairs to knock on the door.

Knock, knock, knock. Laura's hand hit on the door. A pause and then from inside a voice that said, "Come on in. It's open."

When Laura touched the handle to open the door, a spark hit her and a whisper was in her ear, "My love, you have no need for a gypsy. I am willing to answer any questions you have."

She let go and quickly turned around because the voice sounded as if he was standing right behind her, speaking directly into her ear. "Oh shit, I am really and truly going nuts. Now I am hearing a dream when I am fully awake."

"Come in, please," the woman's voice said again from inside, and again, Laura went to open but this time without a spark and entered.

When she did, the instant smell of incense stunned her nose and she almost sneezed but didn't. Adjusting to the dim lighting from the outside sunshine, she saw a very clean and elegantly arranged home with flowers and pictures that hung on every space possible on the walls and rugs on the floors, all of various colors, shapes, length, and styles. Laura thought to herself that she had just walked into Alladin's castle.

The woman's voice was heard. "I am back here in the sitting room. Come on through."

Winding around the furniture and tables that cluttered the room, Laura made it to what the woman called the sitting room and entered. "Hi, I am Valerie, and you must be Laura. I hope your trip here was pleasant?" she asked as she was sitting on the far side of the round table, sipping what smelled like a strong tea.

"Yes, it was fine, thank you," Laura replied. "Honestly, I don't even know why I even called you or what I was thinking."

Valerie just looked at Laura from over the rim of the tea cup and stated, "Well, you're here. Let's just have a go at it for curiosity's sake. What do you think?"

"Well, okay, let's," Laura said as she was sitting on the other chair across the table from Valerie. "How do we do this?"

"First, let me see your right hand."

Laura put up her right arm and held it out. Valerie took it into hers and turned Laura's palm up and, then with her pointer finger, started tracing the lines on the inside of her hand.

"You have had many tragedies in your young life! Your life line shows a strange length of life and death, but then goes on with no seeing of afterlife."

Laura started to say something but Madame Valerie picked up her hand as if to say "hush" and Laura went quiet. "The rest of your palm future is very cloudy as if you have an uncertain decision to make. Now shall we do your tarot reading?"

Madame Valerie took the deck of cards from the table, shuffled them, then placed them back onto the table. "You need to cut the cards as many times as you see fit, please."

Grabbing the pile, Laura out once, twice, three times then placed them back where they were. Valerie then again picked up the pile and started to place one card straight down, then another and another and again, only the next went horizontal to the others and she then placed two more above this. The rest of the cards Valerie pulled went to the sides. Laying the cards deck down, she began to say what each card meant in contrast to each above it.

"Are you sure of this?" Madame asked Laura.

"Why? What do you see? Something bad?"

Madame Valerie started, "You have the Lady-in-Waiting. Are you seeing someone or you could be? The Handsome Prince, the man you are seeing is the person you have waited on or will be in your life soon. The Path to Tranquility, your journey of future or present. Destiny or Jester is a combination of what your future will be or the person in your life is playing you for a fool. Despair, this can go with the destiny and the Jester in which it means, well, let's say a broken promise or broken heart. The Tree of Life, when the decision is made from the above sequence, your life will be Death. This follows the Tree of Life as a new beginning or an end of life."

Sitting there hearing what Madame Valerie was saying but not really comprehending, Laura then, with a shock, asked, "Okay, you're saying that I am going to meet someone but he's going to make me a fool. Then I have a decision to make whether I want or am going to live or die? Now this really sucks!"

Valerie looked at her and, with a very pleasant voice of calmness, told Laura, "Laura, this does not mean that it will happen like I said, only that it could. There are many paths that a person can take. What you decide when the time comes is how the next path will follow."

Laura now understood a little more and smiled and said, "Thank you."

Valerie reached out and held her hand, which gave Laura goose bumps because of the quickness and strength that the hold was on her.

"Before you go, I must tell you, be careful of the man you already know. He brings much sadness and death where he walks."

Laura couldn't believe again how very close to her life Madame Valerie had come to the truth, so getting her hand back out of Valerie's grip, she asked, "How much do I owe you?

Mrs. Valerie shook her head and, without a blink or hesitation, replied, "Not a penny. You will be needing it more than I! Promise me, on your travels you will not forget what I have said."

Laura, giving a startled but thankful look, said, "I won't and thank you." She walked back around the maze of furniture and rugs to the door.

Back outside, Laura wrapped her coat around herself because, though the sun was shining bright, the wind was a killer!

Walking all bundled back to the bus stop her thoughts were kept busy with what was told. It was on this walk Laura made her mind up to go find out more information about the letters, deeds, and especially who this Curtis Cordley was and if he was even a real person.

Getting to the bus stop just as it pulled up, Laura was thankful she didn't have to stand out in the cold for long.

One down, she thought as the chill slowly thawed from her bones, sitting and planning what to do first.

Ding! brought her back to the bus, and almost missing her stop, she rushed off just to almost lose her breath from the rush of cold into her lungs.

"Mummmph, cough, cough," catching was by.

Standing there, buttoning up the outside, she said, "Damn, I can't wait to get home!"

A man with glasses, a short beard, and wearing what looked like a lawyer's coat turned and said, "Excuse me?"

"Sorry I spoke out loud," Laura said back, embarrassed a bit.

She hurried now to get to the comer for the next bus, which, when she turned the corner, was already there, and started to say some choice words, but stopped and said, "It couldn't have been too good to last," meaning the bus stops and time.

Now the walk was only a few more blocks to the exchange and the last bus to home. Laura decided to walk, which turned out to be a stupid idea.

Just as the aloneness started to set in, as the rush of lunch slowed and there weren't many people out, she started to feel the hair on the back of her neck stand up and the sensation of being watched.

It's the middle of the day. Who would be perverted enough to be creepy when the sun was up? Laura thought.

But what startled her was that the feeling she felt was not of being watched but watched from the inside when his voice again was heard by only her ears. As seductive as he was, she was angered as her brain listened, "Your questions that are on your mind I can answer. You only need to ask the right questions. Going to gypsies will only cause you confusion and spending your money that, when you are joined with me, you will need no more. I can—"

"Stop it," Laura said in her mind. "You are driving me crazy or maybe I already am. Just go away and leave me alone!"

CHAPTER

fifteen

Looking down the street she could see the bus and felt a rush of relief as it came closer. She walked up the stairs, paid her fare, and found a seat, which, at this time of the day, was not hard because they were plentiful.

Closing her eyes as she sat in the seat enjoying the semi silence of the bus, Laura's mind began to drift into a number-crunching saga. "How much will it cost to get back to the States? Okay, that's not going to cost. I have an open ticket. No worries there." She remembered now the next numbers: how much was it going at cost for the info of her family line? It's not going to be as easy in the States than here because, as she knew, USA is never free. There's always a charge or a catch.

Then the bell went off, but this was not her stop so she just was almost thankful to hear that obnoxious bell. It brought the thought train back to normal.

Now frilly aware and not lost in whatever someone wants to call it, Laura now sat and just watched the streets go by.

Street by street things started looking familiar until her stop was the next.

She slid to the edge of the seat to get up quick and off she read-ied. But things were not going to go Laura's way today because, as the bus rounded the corner, a car that was traveling the opposite way had lost control just up from them on the hill and was heading right for the bus at a speed any who was watching knew was going to end up in a mess.

As the action was seen through Laura's eyes, time slowed down and a slow-motion film was being played. Then just before the crash, the voice yelled a command, "Laura, you must lie down between the seats. Now, my love!"

Just as the word "love" came out, *Whack, scrape!* The sound of metal tearing and glass shattering was all around. Screaming was also so loud that Laura could not make sense of it all. It felt or seemed like a dream. Only when the noise stopped and darkness overcame her was there peace and silence.

What Laura didn't know was the bus and car were a total mess. The good thing was everyone was alive, including (by only a miracle) the driver of the car because, right before the hit, the car somehow spun around and hit the broadside instead of head-on, making impact spread out. Lucky for him! But the bus driver and the few people who were seated behind him weren't that lucky. They had all suffered many degrees of injuries—none life threatening, but they were hurt.

Laura, on the other hand, had many superficial cuts and bruises, but all in all, when she did wake up, she was told by one nurse, "Ma'am, if it weren't for you lying down and the seats folding up over you keeping you encased, you would have or could have been badly hurt. Those seats saved you. You're a very lucky girl!" The nurse said this, and Laura could only remember the voice before...

After being told she was okay and they were getting the discharge papers ready, she thought, *Now what am I going to do? I am back across town and how am I getting home?*

Getting all her belongings together and the hospital gown off, Laura went out toward the desk to sign the release papers. As she was walking out the double doors to contemplate what to do, her eyes found a wonderful sight.

There in the parking lot was Jamie with another person. Laura, raising her hand in an upward and fistful motion, silently said "yes" and walked over.

"Hey, what are you doing here?" she asked as she got within earshot.

Turning around and seeing who was almost screaming at her, Jamie said in a loud voice, "Girlie, what the fuck you doing here?"

Laura then stood on the other side of the car. "You didn't hear about the bus crash earlier?"

"Well, yeah, but I didn't pay much attention. I was here upstairs with Lenny. He has a doctor's appointment."

When Jamie stopped, Laura looked at him and bluntly blurted out, "Well, asshole, I was on that bus!"

Jamie's eyes about bulged out of his head and he just about jumped over the car and started to pat and search her body for anything that might be hurt. "Shit, are you all right? You're not hurt, nothing broken, and why didn't you call me?"

Feeling bad now, Laura gave her answers. "Yes, I'm all right. No, I am not hurt, just a couple of scratches, and no, nothing is broken, but I do need a ride home!"

Giving her the biggest hug she could ever remember, he, of course, said, "Yes, but I have to take Len home first, okay?"

"Yep, let's go."

Going through town, sitting in the backseat, Laura asked, "So, Lenny, the docs give you a clean slate?"

Lenny and Jamie both turned to each other with a shocked look as if to say, "How do we answer this one," but Lenny turned in his seat as far as the seatbelt would let him and looked her in the eyes to say, "No. He told me I was going to die but he couldn't say when."

"Shit, man, I'm sorry. What's wrong?" Laura replied.

Jamie turned to her quickly and just blurted out, "He's got AIDS."

Laura had nothing to say but the only thing that she could, "Damn, dude. I'm sorry."

Lenny didn't say anything else all the way to his place until they pulled over to let him out. "Thanks, Jamz. I'll call up later."

"I'll be home in about thirty minutes. Talk to you then."

Getting out and into the front seat, Laura looked at Jamie and said, "That sucks, man, yow."

Cutting her off very quickly, Jamie snapped out, "No. I use a condom all the time!"

Nothing more was said until Jamie reached out after taking his hand off the gearshift to put it over hers. "I'm glad you're okay!"

She just turned and smiled then let her hand fall back, closing her eyes until the car parked at their house.

Getting out he asked her if she wanted to come over and Laura declined, stating, "You need to call Lenny and be as supportive as you can right now, but I will talk to you later."

Entering, they both split at the stairwell, Jamie going to his apartment and Laura to hers.

Unlocking the door and entering, Laura's first thought was about making the trip and when, so she got out her telephone book and looked up the number to the bank in California. Looking at the time and seeing it only had about a half an hour before closing she called, keeping in mind the time difference.

"Ring, ring," the earpiece sounded in her ear.

"Good afternoon, Sunlight Bank. This is Jessie. Can I help you?"

"Hi, can I speak to Don Keaton, please? This is Laura Wilds placed on hold."

"Hi, Laura. How are you doing? Long time no hear from you. How is London doing it for you, and what can I do for ya?"

"Hey, Don, and yeah, I am doing okay. London's great except the weather, but the reason I am calling is because I need to get some money out of my trust. Can you wire it to me?"

"Yeah, I can but it won't be until tomorrow. We're almost ready to close."

"That's okay. I will need about five thousand and put another ten in my savings."

Now he has questions. "Laura, why so much and you know the stipulations on how you can spend your money."

"Yes, I know. I am coming back to the States to do some research on my family tree and then I am going to fly over to Ireland."

Don, wanting to ask but didn't, just ended the conversation with "The money will be wired western line and come into the bank when you get here and sign all the papers, okay, sweetie?"

"Okay, Don, and thank you. I'll explain everything when I get there. Bye and good night."

She hung up the phone and felt really shitty. Laura undressed to get into the tub and relax some of the banged up bones she still can feel from the accident. Before getting completely undressed, she started the water and gathered up a few candles, lighting them in the bathroom.

Dropping the pants she had on and testing the water with her fingertips, finding it just right, she slipped one foot, leg, and then the other leg, and holding onto the edge of the tub slid her ass and the rest of her into the warm, soothing water.

When the last movements were needed, an "aahhh" came out as she was feeling very relaxed for the first time in days. Grabbing the sea sponge and body soap Laura began to lather and clean up, starting at her toes and slowly washing to the top of her legs then going to her right arm and switching hands down her left arm, swapping the sponge back to her left and soaping up her breasts and neck area. Then she lay back to cop a short relax before letting the water out and washing her ass in a shower.

Only thing was, she relaxed until she fell asleep and her dreams/nightmares flooded her.

First the crash and a play by play of what happened, what she saw and heard, then what Madame Valerie said—and not what was said but the warning she stated. This didn't last long because her body shocked her back when the water temperature started to get a bit chilled. Opening her eyes, Laura scolded herself. "Damn, I hate it when I do that!"

Sitting up and pulling the plug, she waited until the water was just about gone to start the shower. Turning on hot water first, she stood until cold was needed, then fixed it 'till standing under the streams was just as soothing as the tub.

Getting some more soap, she started to wash what was missed, only as she washed a tranquil feeling came over her and she began to feel the breeze of a warm blow down her neck just under her left ear.

In a stop, her hands halted washing, but she could still feel as if she was being lathered. Not really wanting the feeling to stop, Laura didn't even open her eyes and just let it be.

"That's right, Laura. Let me hold and help you relax. Let me take all your pains and hurts away."

At this time she was so warm and floating that when his hand brushed the mound above her womanhood, all her mind would do was hum, then with a fluid motion, he parted her folds and with two fingers entered her.

A swoosh of euphoria came over her, and feeling his chest behind her, she melted and let him possess her, entering and exiting her with his fingers while the other hand massaged her left breast, bringing her nipple to a hard and wanting more point. The motion of his right hand brought her to the where her legs felt as if they could not hold her weight, and just as if Curtis knew this or could feel her unstableness, he released her breast and wrapped his arm around the waist part of her already excited body, still using his fingers with such a thrusting she came all over his hand.

The juices dripped down the fingers that were still inside her as the muscles he had so professionally awakened pulsed around them. Pulling them out slowly so Laura could feel everything, he exited her just to take those two fingers up to his mouth and insert them as if they were a popsicle, sucking her honey that washed over them as a moan escaped his throat.

His right hand, then completely cleaned from his tongue and lips, gripped her hip while the other gripped the other side and impaled her on his long, thick engorged shaft. This shower became, at this point, her place of escape and her prison. Speaking ever so softly and erotically into her ear, Curtis said but few words, "You will be mine when you return to my beginnings!"

Those words were the last she heard because the next thing she knew, he swelled so big inside her that she felt all her skin stretch and he released in a hot, forceful stream his seed.

Sitting there under the water and not wanting to ever move from the spot again, Laura opened her eyes and she was alone. Despair and a sudden lust came upon her as she washed, rinsed, and got out to dry.

She walked into the bedroom to see a single rose laid upon her pillow that was not there when she entered before. A smile and terror rushed to her. As she could think of nothing but him and the sheets were pulled back and her naked body slid between them alone.

CHAPTER

sixteen

Waking up this morning was a tough one because Laura now started to feel the pull to this ghost, dream, or maybe a demon that has taken space in her life since her mother's death. Thinking back she thought how, when growing up, her mother really didn't have any stay-at-the-house boyfriends. Sure, she went out but never had any come home and stay. Was this the reason? Laura couldn't think like that especially being her mom and having what she had had. "Ukie" came from her lips. But in the back of her mind, she had to find answers and today was the start.

Flinging her legs over the edge of the bed and sudden ouch of hurt, not pain but love-making hurt came on her in her thigh areas. "Oh great, I have sex hurts from a dream. Now I know I am nuts!"

Getting all the way up, she started to gather up the clothes that will be needed at least for a week's time 'cause the rest can be bought when needed. Putting piles on her bed then getting the suitcase that she thought was never going to be needed again on the floor right where she left it, Laura scooped up most of it—photos, letters, and anything she thought might help—and packed them into what room was left on top of the clothes and zipped the bag.

Going back into the bathroom the first thoughts again was the shower but shaking it off and gathering up all the toiletries she just pushed them into the bag she hadn't yet removed since moving in and walked back out, tossing it down on the bed next to the suitcase.

"Now, oh yeah, passport, coffee to drink, checking telephone machine, and oh shit, what am I going to tell Jamie?" All of this in no real order but a simple to-do mind list she started, coffee then Jamie. "No, I will tell him after I go to the teller for the money." Coffee again and a cup was brewing but not fast enough today.

Dressed and a good half a cup already drank, purse in hand, she was off. Making sure to lock the door, Laura was gone. Good thing was the Western line was in any mom-and-pop store so she only had to go four or five blocks, walking distance. It really didn't take long and the girl that opened was just unlocking the door and opened it for her.

"Mornin', ma'am," the cherry eighteen- or nineteen-year-old said.

"Hey," Laura said back, "do you have any wires that came in the name of Wilds come through yet?"

"No, I have to turn the machine on. Want some coffee while you wait? I just made it."

"Yes, please." Laura found a seat at one of the three tables that were inside and waited. The girl brought over the cup of Joe and told her that it will take a minute to get through if there was any and Laura said that she would wait.

Waiting didn't take long because as soon as the machine warmed up, it was cooking with a lot of dings, ruppps, and noise that sounded like typing. The girl looked at Laura and said, "Well, it looks like this is going to be a busy day" and chuckled a little.

"Ms. Wilds, your wire came but I don't have this much. You will have to go to the check cashing place half a block down or if you have a bank—"

Laura cut her off and said, "No, the store is fine." She showing her ID and waited for the girl to fill out the paperwork, which felt like it lasted forever.

Laura was walking down to the place to cash the check, but as she walked, her mind drifted to how she was going to tell Jamie and what was she doing kinds of thoughts. Finding the place pretty easily, but as she entered, there was already a line of five or so people. Laura just stepped in with them.

Only thing that was heard was someone behind the counter with what looked like bullet-proof glass and cameras everywhere, saying, "Next." It was her turn, and as she walked up to the glass, the lady, almost like a robot, said, "ID or passport and please sign the document in sight, please."

Getting out ID and the check and having to ask for a pen, which the woman rolled her eyes to, she signed and waited.

Signing the check with the pen back, the lady said, "Hold on, I have to call on this being it's coming from the States. It will only be a minute."

Coming back to the window, the lady almost had a smile, but Laura could not really tell. She just looked at her without any emotion. "How would you like that, large bills or small?"

Laura answered, "Large, please. Thanks."

The lady counted the stacks of money onto the counter and when completed placed them all into two bill envelopes, gave an almost smile, and said, "Have a nice day. Next."

Laura just shook her head and walked to the door, pushed, and was back on the sidewalk heading home. "London weather really does fucking suck. It is going to be good to get back to sun, fun, and the beach," she said to herself as she walked hurriedly toward home because it was and felt again like the weather was going to get nasty. Getting just up to the corner and rounding it to her apartment block, Laura saw someone sitting out on the steps. She couldn't tell who it was but thought it looked like Jamie but wasn't sure.

Getting closer up she was right, it was him but he didn't look like everything was fine, and sitting down next to him, she asked, "What's wrong because you're never up this early?"

Placing his hands onto his face, he sadly said, "You remember Lenny from last night?"

"Yeah, why?"

"His roommate just called and said he tried to kill himself. They have him in the hospital in psych."

"Oh man, I'm sorry. Was it because of what the doctor told him or need I even ask?"

"Nope, that's it." Jamie, still with his hands on his face, said back, but what he said next really caught her off guard, "Laura, do you think God, or whoever, is pissed off at us gays for being gay and that's why there's an AIDS crisis?"

Laura couldn't think of anything to say except "I have no idea. Sorry, James. But not to put bad news on top of bad, I have to tell you that I am going back to the States today. I have to get to the bottom of this 1800s shit and find out about some letters I found that were to my grandma and mama. I don't know when I will be back but I am coming back."

"What are you going to do with your flat?" he said, dragging his hands away from his face.

"Well, I'm going to keep it and kinda hoped you would watch it for me, please."

"What's next? The sky going to fall?" he said with his always present shitty grin. "Of course I'll watch it for you but you have to leave the keys so I can raid your cupboards."

"Done." And she hugged him and asked if he wanted some coffee.

"Yep, you betcha," which sounded really weird coming from a guy with an English accent. Unlocking again all the locks and opening the door, the smell of fresh coffee was still in the air, and Laura went in to get a couple cups made as she had forgotten to shut the maker off when leaving.

"So what are you going to be doing in America?" Jamie asked.

Now having to tell someone, she started to run down what the fortune teller said and about the letters that had questions. She had to find out the who was, although not telling him kinda new and that she was also going to go to Ireland for more info.

He just sat there and blinked then sipped his coffee and said, "This break-in and fingerprints really has you spooked, doesn't it?"

"Yeah, it does and the detectives can't or won't finish anytime soon so I am. I'll call ya and keep in touch. I promise."

"Cool," he said. "I have to piss, be right back." Jamie went off to the bathroom and came back out with the rose in his hand and the bloom up to his nose smelling it.

"Who gave ya this? It's really pretty and smells good too."

Laura's face, she could feel the color running out of because, like a ditz, she forgot or tried to forget last night. She lied and said, "I bought it when coming from the fortune teller. It made me feel better."

"You mean it made it through the crash?" he said, knowing she was lying, but didn't push it.

He put the flower on the coffee table, and before he said something else, he stood still and excused himself with a "You got a lot to do. Just let me know when you're leaving," and headed for the door.

"Okay, I will." She was actually glad that the push for an answer wasn't there as she rose to lock up after he left.

Going back into the living room and looking up the number for the airport, she dialed and booked a flight to Los Angeles using her Visa card as confirmation, and after hanging up, she tidied up around the place but left everything there so Jamie could use them if he needed to. Then she went into the bedroom to finish and see if she missed something.

Her flight wasn't for hours, but as she already knew, getting there early was a must with the new customs shit and all since 09/11 happened, so picking the suitcase and bathroom bag, she headed out, but as she exited the bedroom, there was the rose, and not knowing why she did, she unzipped the bag and placed it carefully on top and zipped it back up. Remembering to turn the coffee off and wash the cups, she left stopping at Jamie's place to tell him she was leaving.

Hugs and good-byes were exchanged, and she asked him to call a taxi because the bus would take way too long. She went out to wait and he followed not long after. Sitting there waiting felt like hours but she made it. Jamie, on the other hand, didn't say anything and to Laura that was kind of weird all by itself. Then he came out of nowhere with "Why didn't you want me to drive ya?"

She told him the truth, "You're never up at this time and traffic is going to be a mess in about an hour, so I didn't want you in the middle of all the mess."

"Cool" again was all he said. He looked up just in time to see the taxi coming down the street, but this wasn't hers 'cause it stopped just by the corner home and honked a few seconds, then a heavier woman in a dress came out with a large purse and hat to get in. Just as that one waiting, another came up behind it. "That has to be yours," Jamie said.

And they waited. Sure enough, it followed the other and stopped right there in the street. The driver just about blew the horn until he saw the two of them on the stairs with the bags and waited.

Jamie and Laura said good-byes and he helped her in the taxi and watched it drive off sadly.

Laura knew, even as he was a party animal at night, it was day when he was most alone and it made her sad, but she had to do this even if it meant leaving. As they headed down the road, she said to the driver, "To the airport, please."

The driver just nodded with no words. The trip was long and quiet but Laura didn't mind. *Maybe that's a good thing for now*, she thought to herself.

Almost forty-five minutes later, they arrived at the terminal. The driver got out and helped her out handing bags to her as he said, "That will be 24.53 pounds." All she had were dollars so she gave him a fifty and said, "Keep the change."

He smiled and said, "Have a nice flight," as he was backing and sped off.

Eating was the easy part, getting all the gooey and sticky from the bun was another, so getting up to wash this was going to be fun because the restroom was all across the room.

"Great," she said and with one hand gathered everything again as not to get any on her clothes. One good thing about airports, they always have clean bathrooms with soap. Cleaned up and now all full, Laura was ready to wait again when over the loudspeaker it came, "Flight 362 to Los Angeles, California, USA, now boarding gate 32."

"Damn it. Now I have to wait in another line," Laura said.

The line that she thought was going to be a nightmare turned out to be just the opposite. It went quick and with no problems. Walking the sky way, the butterflies started to kick and Laura started to subconsciously think about what was happening and what she was doing or had to do, which was at this point still up in the air. It was a play-as-you-go venture. Boarding the plane and opening the hatch for carry-on luggage, which was always stuffed with other's junk, she sat down, strapped in, and waited for the directions of airways, oxygen masks, emergency exits, and so on and so on.

A voice over the speaker came. It was the captain. "Good day and welcome to Travel Line Flights. We are starting our flight today with good weather and no delays so it should be a smooth flight. Our stewardess Nicole will be showing you about the emergency instructions. Please pay attention and again thank you for flying with us."

Nicole came on right after he ended, and Laura just sat there because all this she has been through before. Every plane says the same thing, just different airlines. The seatbelt light came on shortly after Stewardess Nicole finished and the wheels turned. The plane was moving up, up, up and off the ground she was.

She set her head back and closed her eyes just for a short nap, which only lasted about ten minutes because one of the three stewards was giving out sodas, drinks (adult sodas), and those unforgiving peanuts that stick between your teeth.

Declining all but the drink, Laura ordered a gin on the rocks and some peanuts, but she wasn't going to eat them. The guy next to her asked if she was going to eat them and if not, could he have them so she ordered them and passed them off but had to wait for her drink.

Time passed and the tray came back around. Receiving the drink, she sipped it and placed the tray open from the back of the seat in front and relaxed again.

No such luck! The guy who sat next to her right away started to talk, and Laura just sat and listened to him being polite as she always was.

Before she knew it, the flight was two hours in and a movie started, the one that has a guy going into Egypt and finding treasures but finds the bad guys first.

Thank goodness, when it started, the guy who was beside her shut up because Laura thought by the time they landed he would tell his life story. She closed her eyes again and finally slinked into a sleep with no dreams, no imaginary man making her body come alive, just a sleep.

Only thing that was heard next was the captain letting everyone know they were now entering US air space, and at this time, there were no delays. "Great," she softly said to herself and fell back to sleep.

Waking up and looking at her watch, she had slept for about five hours and looking around saw that most everyone was also sleeping, but a few were working on laptops or reading books.

Laura unbuckled her seatbelt and got up. She had to pee like a race horse and slowly walked up the narrow aisle to the back where, just before getting the door, the hair on the back of her neck stood up and his voice could be heard but only in her head, "Soon, my love, very soon shall we meet."

Pulling the door latch to the toilet, she entered smelling the overpowering odor of chemicals and really bad perfume or aftershave. She pulled her pants down with panties in one push and sat down. A shock on her ass because of the seat gave a chill and the stream of pee flowed. "Ahhhh," Laura said while sitting there. Wiped and washed her hands and read all the warnings on the "Do Not's" of what not to do with the water.

She dried and exited back to her seat, where sitting down and getting comfortable again, she went back to sleep.

seventeen

Waking up with everyone else to a voice saying, "Good morning, we will be landing in about two hours. If anyone would like any breakfast at this time, please leave your choice with one of the stewardesses that will be around momentarily."

Fidgeting in the seat and straightening up as not to wake up Tim, she sat—bored—and waited, trying to stay awake without the convenience of a shower.

"Morning. Would you like anything to eat?" Looking up and saying yes, Laura was informed on what were the choices and requested a bagel with cream cheese then, because her seatmate wasn't up, the stewardess left to the next row of seats and repeated herself.

The bagel was delivered and eaten, which helped in Laura's belly, filling the craving the sticky bun did not. Looking at her watch, there was only about an hour left and the plane should be landing, hopefully.

Since the 911 tragedy, anyone that gets on a plane has a small fear or a moment's thought of going down. If anyone says they don't, well, they are either fearless or just plain lying.

Sure, ran across Laura's mind. The intercom fuzzed and beeped and the captain was on.

"We will be landing in LA very shortly. Please make sure anything that was taken out during our flight is now secure. Please turn off all electrical equipment and put your seatbelt on."

About twenty minutes later, the sound of motors thrusting back and the plane banking to the left could be felt. Seat neighbor Tim, who was now up and looking out the window, turned and said, "This is the best part of flying, seeing all the lights and land colors blow up, don't you think so?"

"Yeah, it's cool, but landing safely is much better," Laura said and Tim gave a slight laugh.

Again looking out he turned and almost as if he was a kid said, "I can see the airport and runway. Here we go!"

Laura just smiled and rolled her eyes. Motion of a roller coaster started to roll up the hill and the erp, erp, swizz, errs rush of the wheels and engine hitting the ground and slowing. She knew it was over.

"Welcome to Los Angeles, California. Please gather everything and exit the plane when we have come to a complete stop, and again, thank you for flying Travel Line Flights. Come fly with us again."

The plane stopped and taxied to a parking area, but this time there were stairs, not a jet way, which sucked as Laura inhaled the beautiful thick smog and unhealthy air of California.

Off the stairs and walking with everyone that was on the plane, they all entered into a terminal that was hopping with people, noise, and more on top of more. Laura smiled and Tim who walked with her said, "Welcome to the good ole U. S. of A." They both laughed then parted and went their separate ways at the end of the corridor.

Almost relieved that Tim didn't turn with her, Laura continued up and into the front area, hoping to catch a cab. Getting closer to the exit doors, she wasn't going to have to wait as there were lines of them double-parked.

Hurrying out and lifting up her arm to beckon one, an older man got out and hurried to her. "Where you want to go, young lady?"

Laura said as she handed her bags to him, "To the Sea Breeze Inn, please."

"Sure enough," he answered while holding the door open for her. As the cab was exiting the airport and getting onto the inter-state, the driver started to ask the normal small talk, "You staying long? Here for business or pleasure? Will you be doing any sightseeing while you're here?"

Laura, being polite, was short with "Not long I hope. Business. And no I'm from here. Seen just 'bout everything a person can see." But she did ask him, "Is this going to be a short ride at this time of day?"

"Yes, ma'am. I will take a couple of shortcuts to help save you some pennies," he said. The rest of the ride was in silence.

After about forty-five minutes, he perked up and let her know they were about a block away and said the toll, which was $42.38. Laura swallowed hard but started to get her money out.

Stopping, he ran around, opened her door, and said, "Have a good day," as she handed him $45. And said, "Keep the change" and walked into the inn to check in.

"Hi, Laura Wilds, I have a reservation."

"Hello, Mrs. Wilds, and welcome. Your room is ready. Do you have your credit card and ID ready?" the clerk asked.

"Yep, and it's miss."

Getting all the info on where the ice machine, restaurant, and pool were, she headed to her room. Entering she dropped her bags and plopped on the bed, clothes and all, fluffing up the pillows and grabbing the remote to see what's on the boob tube. It has been far too long since she saw the whooply of the California streets and all the bad things that go on.

Only as Laura relaxed, her eyes became heavy with jet lag, and before she knew it, she was asleep.

CHAPTER
eighteen

The moment her mind started to drift off, Curtis knew it and he plunged into her mind. First thing he did was to lay next to her while she slept and just watch her until he had to touch her. With his finger, he pushed the hair that hung over her face up behind her left ear and gently placed a kiss on her cheek.

Laura smiled in her sleep and moaned a soft "mmm" as he did this. Then just as on queue he pressed his lips upon hers and lustfully tasted her as she opened and allowed him to do whatever he wanted.

Still in a dream, she opened her eyes to find him looking back and her body jumped with a wanting need. Her mouth watered, her breasts became two mounds of luscious bags that needed to be touched, and the lower part of her body was having a breakdown with need, the need to have his body on her and in her.

Then it happened, a very loud and close truck horn sounded as if it was parked in her room, and Laura jumped into a sitting position of unexpected fright taking the dream with it.

Realizing what just happened, Laura surprised herself with saying, "Damn, that would have been…" And then she thought, *It was a dream and this is oh too creepy!* Seeing that the TV said it was almost eight in the evening and she hasn't even started on anything that she needed yet. "Well, it's too late to start calling anyone so I might as well get some chow."

Reaching over the bed and sprawling it to reach the other side and the telephone, Laura noticed the warmth of the blanket where in her dream he was lying next to her, and her mind hesitated only for a moment then continued fumbling with the phone.

Grabbing the cord and pulling, she got it onto the bed and reached for the phonebook. "Pizza. Naw, okay Chinese. Yep, that's it." So looking under take-outs, she called and ordered.

Grabbing the remote and sitting there channel-surfing, she waited, finding an old horror movie.

"Knock, knock. Take-out," a person said at the door. Getting up and getting her purse she looked in the peep hole and there was an oriental man with a bag waiting, so opening the door and paying the guy with a thanks, she took the food, locked the door back up, and sat down to chow.

Getting full and laying back down Laura felt tired again, so keeping the TV on for company, she got undressed and covered up. "No dreams this time," and she slept.

CHAPTER
nineteen

"Ring, ring, ring," the phone was going off. When answered, it was the front desk.

"Ms. Wilds, good morning. It's ten thirty. Will you be staying with us again?"

"Oh, I'm sorry. I didn't tell you when I checked in. Yes, I will be here for at least a week. Thank you."

"Please forgive the call and will you be needing any wake-ups for the rest of your stay?"

"Yes, every day around ten, please." Hanging up and getting up with a yawn she went to her bag to get the shower stuff and headed for the bath.

Staying in there for what felt like forever she turned the water off.

Grabbing a towel, drying off, and walking into get her clothes, she stopped dead in her tracks because laying there on the bed was a bright red rose.

Staring at it she walked over to her bag. Maybe she had taken the one out, but looking there, it was right where she left it and now there was another. Picking theflower up and smelling it, she quivered a bit, but now it wasn't freaking her out. Well, she couldn't really answer that and placed this one with the other.

Dressed now, she thumbed the phone book for the nearest place that could or maybe have any records of birth, death, etc. Finding one that wasn't far, she called a cab—it's cheaper and safer here in the States to do—and made arrangements.

Before leaving, she remembered to grab her letters so she could put dates and times with what she found, stuffed them into her purse, and left to the front office to wait.

Cabs here didn't take long because there are thousands of them, and here was hers, taking only about twenty minutes.

"Radio said you wanted to go to Life Lines and Family Trees on Bylee Street, right?" the cabbie said with a strong Indian accent.

"Yes, that's the place."

This ride took her not far, taking about ten minutes, and she was there.

"Four fifty, please."

She handed him exact change and got out. Standing in front of this store that hopefully was going to help, she entered.

She found an office-looking place on the inside with some desks, countertops that went on forever, and some really big tables that looked like x-ray machines but not on the wall.

An older-looking lady got up and gestured her to come around. Laura did and as she got closer the woman said, "Hi, I'm Angela. What can I help you with?"

"Well, I'm trying to look up some information on my family," Laura replied.

"Sweety, you're in the right place. What ya got there and we can get started?"

Handing Angela the papers from the library in London and the letters (only a few) from her grandmother and her mom, she looked and said, "That's all I got. Do you think it's enough?"

"Well, let's see what's in this pile and what I can get out of the computer. Just a couple of questions?"

After about twenty minutes of answer or trying to, they walked over to a computer screen and Angela started to type in the answers into all the boxes. Turning to Laura she said, "This might take a while. Do you want to go do some shopping or something while the computer searches?"

Slapping her knees and giving a thumbs-up, Laura exited, but before opening the door, she yelled, "How long, do you think?"

"I should take about three hours unless there's a hitch with a name or date, but we'll cross that when it happens," Angela shouted back.

She stood on the sidewalk and now had to call Don and let him know she made it. Walking up the street she found a pay phone and swiped her card, dialed, and waited for someone to answer.

Today was her lucky day because Don himself answered, so she let him know where she was and staying and what time was good to come in and sign everything.

Replying, he told her that tomorrow wasn't good. He had meetings, but the mid-day would be great, so a time was set and she hung up.

As Laura hung up a thought came, "I have a full day of nothing to do," so she started to think. "Damn, if James was with me, I could take him sight-seeing," but since she was alone and from here, it wouldn't be much fun. She thought again, *Got it. The museum.*

So she was going to go in the morning and made a day of it. Having about two hours left, she just wandered around, window-shopping and people-watching, which, in no time, took up those couple of hours, and she started to head back to the office and hopefully more answers.

The walk back was okay except California was unpredictable with the weather, and it started looking like there was a storm brewing, so not having any jacket or umbrella, she hurried, making it inside just as the ceiling let loose and rain poured down.

"Perfect timing," Angela said. "I just got done about thirty minutes ago. Wanna have a see?"

Sitting down Angela first showed her some papers with type on it about her mom and the places she lived and herself being born, the when and where of information. Then she started to get into her grandma and the information that was being told. Laura knew only bits and pieces of her grandfather to whom she never met because he had died many years before. Actually before her mom was old enough to know him.

She said he died in 1963. Her mom was only about a year old and then the weirdness got even weirder because the research showed that every mom or daddy in the family died when any child was just a young'un.

Then Angela asked a strange question, "Laura, did you know that there are no boy children in your family tree?"

Laura looked at her with wide eyes and, with a shaky voice, asked, "What … what do you mean no boys?"

"I mean that everyone in your history—and it goes back to 1868 with your great, great, great, great-grandma—they all were married and had children, but none of the records have any males being written of birth, just females, and the stranger part is all the husbands or fathers all died before the kids were two years old. Not to get too personal, but how did any of these women care for themselves and the child without having a man around?

"We, or I, did find some papers that the name Cordley kept popping up, and as I can see whoever this family was or is has paid for everything after the man died."

Laura, now really freaked out, asked a polite but subtle question, "Did anything in my family have anything to do with Ireland?"

Angela looked at her and fumbled with the papers, then turned one over and handed it to her without speaking.

Taking a moment to look it over, Laura looked up at Angela and, with hesitation, asked, "My family line of the girls came from there? When? There are no dates or cities?"

"No, there isn't, but I did make a couple calls and the people we work with over there can help you if you want to travel."

As she was saying this, she passed a note with an address and phone number to her. "Her name is Odell McPherson and she's expecting your call."

"I actually was planning on going there and thank you for your help. How much do I owe you?"

"Hold on. Let's go up to the front and I'll get your receipt."

She gathered up all the papers and walked up with Angela, who now was punching numbers on the calculator. "Total, Laura, is $139.42. That's our research fee and for the copies."

"You take VISA, right?" Laura asked, handing her card over.

"Yep, sure do. Hold on for your receipts and thanks for using our services. Let anyone you know about us, and Laura, good luck," Angela said with a smile.

Signing her name and having the papers, Laura walked out, now finished with the hard stuff, and headed back toward a coffee shop she had seen earlier.

Ordering a drink and asking for a phone, she walked out and went to the corner where the kid said a pay phone would be. She got the change from her pocket and called the cab company that she used earlier for a ride back to the inn.

twenty

Arriving at the motel or inn, she went inside to find the message light blinking on her telephone. "Mmm, I got a call?" Ringing the front desk and requesting the note, it was from the bank and one of his meetings was cancelled so he was available at three thirty or four o'clock in the afternoon. "Thank you," she said to the clerk and hung up.

Glancing at the house clock, it was now one thirty. "Shit, I have just enough time to shower."

Calling Don and affirming the time, she hopped into the water, did a once-over, and was out. Now dressing like a streak of lightning, she called back the cab and headed out to the front to wait.

As she was sitting there, his voice was again in her head, speaking ever so softly, almost tenderly. "You will soon be where my blood runs and I can show you many delights that no one else can."

"Woo, that really freaks me out when that happens," Laura said to herself as the cab pulled up. Getting in, saying where to go again, she was off, and the next thing on the list, since her stay has now been officially cut by a couple of days, is to find a flight to Ireland and finish this wild goose chase, so she's having a conversation with herself in the cab.

Pulling up to the bank, paying the cabbie, and getting out, Laura remembered the last time she had to come in here, the day papers needed to be signed from her mother's death.

A small chill ran up her spine as she remembered opening the door, walking up yet to another counter.

"Hi, I'm here to see Don!"

"Yes, ma'am, he's expecting you. Have a seat and I'll call him."

Not more than a minute passed and he was out, walking up and giving her a great big hug, one that felt secure and much needed.

"Laura, honey, how have you been? You shouldn't stay away for so long!"

"I'm sorry, Don. It was just too hard to stay with everything that's happened and all!"

"It's okay, sweetie. You are okay though?"

"Yes and no, but I'll make it."

"Well, let's go into my office and take care of what you need."

The two of them headed down the hall and into his officer where they both sat and Don commented, "You know your mother was a real good person. I still miss her coming in with you when she came in, and you have grown into a fine young lady. I know she is proud!"

"Thanks, Don, and she never told me that she wasn't, even when she was in the hospital. Even though she didn't say anything, I could feel it. It means a lot from you too."

"Well, you're welcome and don't ever hesitate to call if you need anything, promise?" He smiled and handed her some papers. "Sign them and we'll go up front and get your money to get you where you're going."

"Yepsedaisy, thanks again."

Heading out of the bank and asking if he'd call a cab, she stood just about where she was let off and waited.

The ride home or to the inn was a little scary, having all the money, but Laura was smart. She put four thousand on a VISA card and only had a grand in her purse, but it was still California and anything could happen.

Getting in to the room, she let out a relaxed exhale for making it without any problems. She picked up the phone and called the airlines to book a flight over to Ireland. Taking about a half hour with all the new security and questions a person had to answer, Laura was glad that was done. Before hanging up the person told her to be there at least two hours early to be on the safe side. "Okay and thanks. Good-bye."

Now having the rest of the night and half the day left, she asked herself, "What do I do?" when his voice came from nowhere.

"Laura, my love, just lay back and rest. I will take up the time you have left. Lay back, my sweet."

With that suggestion, her eyes were laying heavily and she did just as he said. She lay back.

Taking only a moment for him to project himself there beside her, he began by just lying next to her and allowing his body to warm and blend with hers as he rubbed the side of her body she wasn't laying on.

Massaging around her shoulders and the area of her hips he knew when her body was relaxing, in which more could be done. Slowly his hands traveled the length of her body, and ever so softly, he put his hand under the shirt Laura was wearing. Tenderly his fingers began to travel over and around each of her breasts as she exotically moved under them, moving with his hands. Then when her breasts were awakened, he trailed down her cleavage over the flat and wanting mid-section to the band of her jeans. Then, like a professional, he unbuckled the belt, unsnapped, and pulled the zipper down until there was more than enough room to allow his hand to explore her perfectly formed womanhood that he now claimed as his.

Rubbing back and forth under the waistline of her panties, he delved his fingers into and over the bud of feminine quality and through the now-swollen lips of the outside walk of her center. Taking two fingers and spreading them to allow access for a third that now laid at the moistened opening of her well-lubed love canal, he entered slowly, and as he did, Laura moaned a sensuous "mmmm," as she wetted her lips with her tongue, and he leaned over and placed his to hers as he entered and exited her with his finger.

Kissing her made him feel so alive. He inserted another finger along with the one and now was impaling her with two, which made his hips buckle a bit from the insertion but she was getting ever so much more wetter as he plunged.

Laying there with all his clothes on was becoming very uncomfortable because his penis was so full and engorged. It about busted through the seams he was wearing. Stopping what he was doing with his hands, he stood up and shed the clothes he had on, unleashing the long, thick organ that was trapped with a spring. Lying back, he started to slowly take off Laura's clothing, one piece at a time, memorizing again every inch of her body.

After getting her completely naked, he turned her onto her stomach and started rubbing her neck, back, buttocks, and then as she lay sprawled out, took the shaft, and rubbed it along the crack that divided her cheeks.

Slowly up and down he traveled with it in his hand, pushing more and more into the warmth of her back side, going from the spot of moisture up to the split and back until all her was slick, then placing the tip of him against her, he slowly entered her, allowing the muscles to adapt to his size and pushing more inch by inch, stopping for her body to adjust until he was in to the front of his ball sack touching her hot flesh.

Reaching around, he dwelt his hand into her hot honeycomb and, with his two fingers scooped up some natural lube, spreading it onto and around her hole and his length. Now the movement became more of a rhythm than a trial, and pushing her hips up, he filled her with every push, feeling her now getting accustomed to his size until he was ready to spill. Then he exited and re-entered her where he just began to pound harder and deeper than he would in the other.

Laura gave out a loud and sensual scream the moment her inner muscles grasped him and that was it. He expelled everything he held in one long, hot stream deep into her, holding her tight to him until they were both done and all twinges ceased.

Turning her over and kissing her mouth with such love, he got up, dressed, and covered her so she would not get chilled in the night and planted in her mind a suggestion of slumber and pleasure. He left her mind for another day soon to come.

The rest of her slumber was serene and calm, and even when waking, she didn't feel as if a violation had occurred as this was her first experience of having anal sex, even though it was a dream. Or was it? Because when showering, her body felt different in regions that never have been explored until last night, but they weren't hurting, just a worked feeling. She stood there in the tub, letting the hot water run down her body and over the parts that ached but didn't in a way that she about liked it.

After, the water made her body at ease and awake. Realizing she still had almost a day to wait and hang out, Laura decided to stay in and order out, so dressing in only her robe, she hopped back onto the bed, picked up the phone, and ordered from the kitchen some eggs, bacon, toast with jelly, and half an orange. No need for coffee because there was a maker in the room.

Flicking through the channels she found one of those nature programs and stopped. "It's better than cartoons and news," she said to herself and waited for room service.

About half an hour later, there was a knock on the door and a voice, "Room service for Ms. Wilds."

"Hold on," she replied, fastening the robe.

Opening the door, the smell of food penetrated her nostrils and she became even hungrier.

"Please sign here," the bell hop asked.

After closing and relocking the door, Laura sat down at the small table to eat.

After eating and brushing her teeth, glancing at the clock, which Laura knew not to do because it only made time pass slower, she decided to just lay back down and hope Curtis came again.

She was beginning to enjoy this strange and unnatural thing that was happening to her. Laura started to wonder in the back of her mind if this was the same thing that happened to her mom and grandma, then a chill came and even thinking of it really gave her the creeps. Like anyone sitting doing nothing, Laura's body slowly began to go into a slumber mode, and soon, she found herself back asleep with the memory of what happened before and wishing it to happen again but it didn't. She only slept.

Sleeping was what she did almost all day and into the night because, when Laura woke up, the television was doing the static noise and nothing was on. Plus it was very dark outside, which, in the city, wasn't really dark at all.

Finding the remote and surfing, there wasn't anything on unless a person wanted to buy the pay-per-views and that she didn't want, so getting out of bed and opening her luggage, ruffling through it, she found the book she packed and headed back to lay down and read.

Laura has always loved to read. Books always can take a person from problems or even let one's mind relax enough to think and that was what she needed to do—think.

She thought of her agenda and what do to first—research through papers, not only property but blood lines of him, and traveling to any and all places the information took her.

The flight was still some hours away, so reading as much as her eyes would allow, she laid the book down and rolled over to get a short nap, like she hasn't slept enough! But sleep again took her.

CHAPTER

twenty-one

Curtis was where he lay in the times that he's not wandering alone in time and wondering what he was going to do when Laura actually was here, because projecting himself was very strenuous and the pleasure he did felt good but they were only projections and the thought of feeling her body under him in the flesh made him ponder why his emotions felt as they did when it came to Laura Wilds.

Just as her mother, grandmother, and her mother, he was with them, but Laura drew and touched a part of him that he only felt some hundreds of years ago, when his body could feel the warmth of the sun and a tall glass of ale. But now and as it had been since the day he made that one manish mistake and became the thing he is today! He remembered that chilly afternoon in 1773 while on the back of his red-and-white–colored stud, hunting for deer on his family's land near the brook they called the Devil's Water. It was named because it was always hot water that ran in this flowing brook.

To Curtis, hunting deer was a merit because he always came back with enough meat to get through a few more days, unlike today where food is practically made for a person. When he was a young man, everyone hunted and farmed or they starved, but as he rode today, something was not right because he had not seen anything except a few scattered birds flying. Oh yes, there was plenty of signs that meat was here, but none moving and approaching Devil's Water, when a strange wagon was up under some trees he saw, dismounting his stud and investigating. There was no one on it.

Then in his ears, he heard the sounds of singing. A woman's song and it grew louder as he came closer to the water, slowing as not to make any noise so he could surprise anyone. He pushed aside a bush to get a look at who and how many people were on his land.

To his amazement, he was shocked to see a beautiful dark-haired maiden washing herself in the water, alone.

Stepping out from where he was hidden, the woman heard a twig snap and turned, covering herself with her arms so she did and saw him and he her.

She started to scream and Curtis placed his finger up to his mouth as if to say "Be quiet."

She stopped and just gazed at him. Curtis asked her what she was doing.

She replied, "Crossing to visit my grandmother in a village about a day's travel more." She was moving out of the water as she spoke and he, being the loosely male he was, began to feel a wanting from beneath his skin's flap.

"Now, woman, you know this is my land you travel and you have no permission to do so! There is payment to be offered for this trespass."

She looked at him now in fright, knowing in these times what men wanted, and she said, "I have gold. Will you take that?"

Bringing his hand to his chin and rubbing, he said, "We will see. First show me."

She walked over to her clothes and put them on quickly as not to seem vulnerable. He then let her pass to go to the wagon and fetch this gold she said she had and he followed.

Climbing into the wagon and turning, she handed him a leather pouch heavy with the gold she said, but Curtis, being the heir to a small kingdom and doing much what he wanted, jumped into the wagon with her and, with a lusty look, grabbed her shoulders, knocking her to the bottom, holding her flat with one hand, and began to pull up her skirt above her hips.

This girl, even fighting with everything she had, was no match. He was twice as tall and that stronger, but she fought giving him a deep scratch on his left upper arm, and this enraged him to where now instead of being nice, he just took what he wanted.

After he had finished this molestation and looking at her laying there innocent, he looked down at himself, and there was blood on his manhood, on her upper thighs and the floor boarding of the wagon. In shock, he said, "You're a virgin?"

"Yes, you pig. I was until you took what was not yours to take!" Now crying with a soft sniffle, she looked at him with hatred and said, "My grandmother will curse you for what you have done to me, curse you!"

And Curtis, not knowing what to do, just cast her away, leaving the gold and saying, "Wench, get off my land. Go to your grandmother. She can do nothing to me!" He exited and mounted his horse and rode off not thinking twice of what he had done.

That's how men treated women in those days. A week had passed and he really didn't think about that day until a wagon pulled up with about four or five large men, an old woman all dressed up as gypsies.

The butler answered the hate that requested the master of the home and Curtis's father came to the request. "What is it that I have to stop my business?"

The old woman, then angrily speaking, told him what had happened and that justice was to be done.

Upon hearing this, a loud yell could be heard throughout the halls. "Curtis, you travel to the door now!" Getting out of his bed that he had been in all day after a drunken stupor the night before, he ran to the front and at the top of the stairs he saw the girl standing there. His eyes widened and he was now slightly scared as her words came back to haunt him. The only thing he heard in his ears was "My grandmother will curse you for what you have done."

His feet would not move until again a loud, manly yell was heard. "Curtis M. Cordly, move your arse down here!"

Feet started to just about run on top of each other with those words and he was at the bottom of the staircase before he knew it, standing there with no difference his choices were now.

Her brother, looking at him with a stern and unhappy look, said only three words, "Is it true?"

Knowing the reason, all Curtis could say was "Yes."

Without waiting for anyone to say a word, the girl's grandmother raised her fingers into the air and said, "From this night forth, you shall see no sun. You shall live off the fluid of others that you will have to take from for what you have taken of my granddaughter, till the day a young maiden's heart will give to you from her heart."

With that, the family left and spoke no more. The doors closed and questions now were of abundance.

"Why would you? How could you?" and "You have brought shame to oneself for one moment of time when so many would have given freely."

Curtis just had one thing to say, "Do you think the grandmother was serious? Am I cursed?" No one could answer him although, in those days, they believed curses were real.

His day was normal until it was time for everyone to gather around to eat the evening meal.

Curtis, sitting down and piling food onto his plate, started eating as he normally would until his stomach started to wretch and feel as if it was on fire. Excusing himself from the table, he went outside just in the nick of time, for everything in his belly to come out, making his stomach feel even worse.

Wiping his mouth with his sleeve and feeling like someone had beat him up, Curtis went to his room to lay down.

Staying in bed for the next two days, he got up early and ventured out into the morning sun, but the moment its rays were up upon his skin, he felt tremendous pain and backed into the shadows, yet even there, he felt the pain.

Turning into the hallway and being famished from hunger, Curtis headed to the kitchen when one of the maids was walking toward him. All he saw was her and the beating of her heart on the vein that was on her neckline.

Stopping her and knowing she was smitten with him, he led her astray and into one of the room that was within the hallway, closing the door behind them, he proceeded to caress her until they were

94

both breathing very hard, and pulling up her skirt, he started to bring her breathing to a point, just before her explosion.

He bent down and snuggled her neck when from the inside of his mouth he could feel his teeth grow and become very sharp. Opening his mouth and sucking the maid's neck, he pounced. At the same time her release ran down his fingers and into the palm of his hand, warm and sticky. But the warmth and sweetness that ran into his mouth was what brought himself to the brink, the brink of the beginning of his new life as he was now a creature of the night.

CHAPTER

twenty-two

When Curtis finished, he didn't realize that what he had done was drain the poor girl of her life as she was now limp and very dead in his arms.

Panicking within himself but feeling very satisfied, he now tried to think. "What do I do with her body?"

Laying her down on the floor, he covered her with anything and everything until he could rid himself of the body, hoping no one would enter this room until then.

When the sun went down and he could go outside, the first thing was to start a large fire that would look normal, because he was always standing at night with one either cooking a deer or just staying warm. Then the thought of how he was going to bring her out with no one seeing, remembering everyone except for a small staff was here and knowing they were already in bed, he proceeded to retrieve the body.

Entering the room and rolling her into a large rug he had hidden her under, he carried the roll outside and threw her and rug together onto the top of the fire.

Watching as the rug burnt and then the smell of burning flesh drifted into his nostrils. "Oh, dear God, what have I become?" he asked himself.

Now vowing never to bring death to another being and never to burn anyone else, he told himself that he would only take what was needed! And that's what he did until the day came when his family and servants began talking about how he wasn't changing yet everyone else was growing older, grayer, and the change of day into night life.

These were the last days he would see his family. A tear came to Curtis's eyes as he remembered all of this but yet to his uncontrollable destiny, it was as it is.

CHAPTER
twenty-three

Laura, now awake fully and having everything packed, ready and waiting, just sat on the end of the bed and waited as she pushed the channel button, watching absolutely nothing really. The phone rang and it was the front desk letting her know that the cab was here to pick her up. "Okay, be right there."

Doing the run-through in case anything was forgotten, she grabbed the handle of the suitcase and her purse and headed out, turning off the light as she exited, habit from her mom.

Walking down the walkway to the front, instantly the butter-flies started and a tightness in her womb began. *Strange*, she thought. Butterflies, yes, but the other was too freaky.

Shrugging it off the cabbie put her luggage into the trunk and got into the driver's seat. Off they went, but she couldn't get the feel-ing of wanting off her body's mind.

Arriving at the airport just about an hour and half early, as in all ports now for security reasons, Laura made her way into line to wait with everyone else.

She felt like it was taking forever because the check crew was going through everything on top of having people taking off their shoes and even some going into segregated rooms.

Finally her turn was next, and as everyone, Laura had already taken off her shoes, had everything loose in a tray, and was ready. Walking through the metal detector was no sweat, through the pat down and luggage into and out of the x-ray. She gathered everything up and headed to her departure gate.

Sitting there watching all the people unload and board all the planes, run around some knowing where they were going, and some so lost they looked like deer caught in a car's headlights, she waited and waited some more.

The loud speaker beeped and a man's voice called, "Flight 310 to Dublin, Ireland, boarding at gate 12."

Being at the gate already, all Laura had to do was get her ticket torn and get on the plane.

This was something she was getting very used to. Finding her seat and putting the only bag she had other than the purse she hung onto into the rack above, Laura sat down, slightly hoping no one would be next to her.

Watching the people board and most walk by or stop short before her row, she started to relax more and more and really did a slouch when the door was closed and still no one was beside her. "Thank God." Laura exhaled.

Feeling the wheels and engines start with the normal repetitive "Hi and welcome, blah, blah, blah," grabbing the book that was in her purse, Laura started to read.

When she glanced up from the words that were now starting to run together, the window had the most pretty sight, she thought.

Under the plane was the Pacific Ocean with all its bright blues and green colors and sparse glittery specs of tiny little boats floating on what looked like a very calm sea. Above, the sky almost matched the blue of the water and scattered clouds that changed shape as a person watched.

She was thankful for a smooth ride and better day. Relaxed now and feeling a bit sleepy from reading, Laura let herself drop into sleep. Not even waking for when the stewardess came around with refreshments.

The only thing Laura remembered when opening her eyes after the thoughts of clouds was the person behind her shaking her right shoulder and telling her that they were getting ready to land.

She slept the whole trip. Groggily waking and making sure all her stuff were still together, Laura managed to get to the bathroom and pee, which she thought sitting there on the stool would never end, when over the speaker came, "We will be landing in about thirty minutes. Please return to your seats and fasten your seatbelts."

Hurrying now to get her pants up and wash, she came out being the only person up, making her feel the center of attention. Blushing, she sat down and waited. Sounds of the plane's engines going onto reverse and slowing down, then the *erp, erp, erp* of the tires touching the runway, she knew the flight was done and her journey was yet to begin.

The plane came to a complete stop and the doors opened. Everyone started exiting. Laura waited because she hated being in the cattle run lines. One of the last to get out, she thanked the attendants and went down the staircase into customs. She thought, Why do they had to do customs going and coming? Like where would or what would have changed in luggage fifteen thousand feet in the air?" She just chuckled and stood in line.

"Passport, please," a red-haired freckle-faced young man asked. "Are you here for business or pleasure?"

Laura stated both and the man wrote this down with a couple check marks beside some lines of words. He handed her passport back with a toothy smile and a dominant Irish accent. "Enjoy your stay, missy!"

Smiling back, she walked onto the entrance to hail a cabbie. Getting one straight away, the cabbie asked where she was going.

"The Four Leaves Inn on Macintosh Road."

"I know the place. It won't be a long ride." He was right. The ride didn't take long and they were there. He helped bring the bag in. She paid him, then checked in. The clerk behind the desk took the card Laura had entered her information and, with a puzzled look, asked, "Ms. Wilds, I think you have a package. Please wait here a moment." She left Laura and went into the back room to return with a long slender white box in her hand.

Laura quickly asked, "Who is it from?"

"It was delivered earlier this morning without a note, just an invoice with your name and when approximately you would be arriving."

Laura gave her credit card and retrieved the package. She waited for her room key, with question of opening this package in her room.

An explanation of where her room was and all the extras of the inn ending with an "enjoy your stay" let her go on. Coming off the elevator and fumbling with the key as her hands were full, she finally made it in and was really pleased to see the room, which was very pastel and very clean. She dropped everything except the package onto the bed, sat down, and slowly undone the tape that held the box closed. Pulling the top off, her breath caught somewhere between the lungs and the mouth. Laura just stared at a long-stemmed, very bright, and beautiful red rose with a tied yellow bow wrapped around the stem. Seeing a small card in the box she opened it and read:

My Love Laura

My home and lands are yours for the taking.

C.M

Dropping the card from her hand, Laura couldn't believe what she read. This man—err... dream, shadow of her deepest fantasies—was real? She now was breathing again and more determined to find the information she desperately was looking for, but her mind thought a quick "is information or is it love"? She was now torn with wanting and needing.

She laid the box and opened up her suitcase, getting out the papers that had all the places and names and numbers that she already connected with searching information. She called the one that Angela gave her, Odell McPerson. She waited for someone to pick up the phone and ended with a machine. Leaving her name and number of the room Laura hung up. Hearing a growl come from her stomach and realizing she hadn't eaten since before the flight, her hands went to straightening her clothes and heading back down the stairs to the lobby(easier to go down than up),through it and into the dining hall the clerk spoke about and the chicken. Seeing it was almost empty and open, Laura found a seat and waited for a waiter or waitress. Ordering a bowl of stew and some garlic bread with a glass of water, she waited again, not long though because they were out in minutes with the order.

Eating and gazing around the place, Laura felt almost a longing to have someone sitting with her. When at the moment that thought run in her mind, his voice said, "We will be together soon and I will be your companion almost forth." Dropping the spoon into the bowl with a splash that was loud enough for a waiter to turn and look, she blushed and cleaned up the spot that splashed then grabbed up a piece of bread to exit. Shock was still within her from Curtis being in her mind. She got that chilly spine feeling again. Retreating back up into her room Laura took off her top that now had stew splatter on it, placing it in the sink to soak, hoping the stains would come out. She got her bag, getting another top out and slipping it on of course having to change jeans as a woman must do.

twenty-four

Checking the time and seeing it was still early, she lifted up the receiver and dialed Mrs. McPherson's number, hoping she would be there this time. *Ring, ring.* "Hello. McPerson residence."

"Hi, Mrs. McPherson, my name is Laura Wilds. Angela gave me your name and number," Laura introduced.

"Yes, dear, she called me right after you left her place and told me you have a very interesting line you are searching." I have started on the research and already have quite a few pages for you to look at." Now with an excitement in her voice, Laura replied, "Yes, yes, I would. When can we meet?"

Mrs. McPherson told her tomorrow would be better and set a time for three-ish in the afternoon. Hanging up Laura saw that she had almost a whole day until their meeting so out loud she perked, "It's sightseeing time!"

Grabbing her purse and key and making sure everything was there, out the door she went. First stop was the front desk for brochures and some local info. They told her about some tours that weren't on any maps. "That sounds cool." So getting directions and being told the bus lines that would be the best ways to go, she exchanged bills for coins and headed out. Following directions and what buses to take she made it to the first one.

From the window looking out, it was huge, a real blown castle, and Laura's insides felt as if she was ten years old again. Getting off the bus and walking up the stone walkway, the sign read:

Home of Sir Regand St. Riley
Guardian of Our Shores
Defender of Our People

As Laura read she wondered about the dates and all his greatness and if he knew this voice known as Cordley. That was just a thought and with everyone else in the crowd, they entered through the two large wooden doors of his home. Entering she could feel her eyes grow wider at the size of this room the door was opened into. "Wow" was all she could muster to say, yet Laura wasn't the only one. Most of the folks in her little group looked just as wowed. A lady dressed in the turn-of-the-century clothing began to speak and tell the story of who Sir Regand St. Riley was, what he did, and why he did it. It was all very interesting, but what Laura heard and retained was the part she said of the clans or families that ruled these lands. No, his name was not said, but it did give her the question to ask when the tour was done. Exiting this room and into another and another, heading down hallways, up staircases that made the ones in modern buildings look like Legos, Laura just couldn't believe the vastness of how people lived and the artworks that adorned every inch of space on each wall.

Finally after feeling like she had walked alone, the group ended back at the entrance where it had begun. Almost everyone was exhausted except for the smaller children who really didn't care what went on. Seeing that the bus was already there or maybe never left, Laura, with many others, clambered back into their seats and sighed with relief to be off their feet. She thought, *I sure hope not all these tours are like this one!* Sitting back and relaxing she pondered on going on another tour since it was only early afternoon. The bus let everyone off where they got on and a "what the..."came to mind with "don't have anything else to do."

Reaching into her purse for that piece of paper the clerk wrote tours on, she did the ole mini, Minnie, Moe and picked one. This one was somewhere in the next village and she first had to catch three buses. Walking down to the intersection, a lady showed her where the bus link was so she sat down and waited.

Finding the conversations amazing not for the content but the accents in which Laura thought sounded really cool, she just sat listening. Seeing everyone stand Laura too stood up. Yep, it was the #5, the one she wanted. She stepped up, paid her coins, and sat down by a window seat again so she could sightsee without hurting her feet this time. As the bus rode down and around the roads, Laura couldn't help but wonder because some of the buildings looked like the ones in fairy tales and the land was so green with fluffs of white spotting each hill. These were sheep but it was still pretty.

Feeling the bus slow down and having to change to another, she repeated this action only once more to the last stop. This stop, when she got off, the bus was by sight entering into a post card. There were no buildings that didn't belong and less people she has ever seen. It was like going back in time, except for the jeans and T-shirts some were wearing. Staying at the bus stop and again looking at the paper, Laura read that she had to get over to one of the shops on this same road and sign in, so looking around she did see it only because of the wooden sign above the door: Heidi's House of Spirits, which turned out to be a soda-bar combo. Entering Laura was greeted with smiles and hellos.

She asked where she has to sign for the tour. The girl behind the bar, with a sad look on her face, told her the tours didn't go anymore. The man who did them passed away and he hadn't been replaced yet, then she told Laura even worse news. All the buses had stopped for the evening. The one she was on was the last until morn. "Shit," Laura said. Now what? Where can she stay until them? An old man who was sitting at the bar turned to her and, with a very yellow teeth, smiled wickedly and said, "You can come home with me, lassie." Laura shivered not by the remark but by his unpleasant looks and politely said, "No thanks." The girl looked sternly at the man, swatting him with her towel and saying, "Now, Mr. Liam, leave the lass alone!" Turning back to Laura she let her know she had a place her aunt worked at and it was only a block away. She told Laura she would call to let her aunt know that she was coming and, giving directions, turned to make the call. Laura then asked if they took Visa and the girl said no but she could pay here at the pub and show the receipt when she arrived.

Leaving the bar and walking the sidewalk Laura suddenly felt out of place, if not aware she was a stranger in a foreign country. Wrapping her arms around herself, she felt a little better, but not much. Hurrying now she got to the door but didn't have to open it. A large lady stood there as if calling children in for the night. Smiling, she spoke, "Lassie, I was watching to make sure you got here safe. We got some hound dogs of men that prowl this late.

"Thank you for watching and for the room! I was to show you my receipt."

"Don't worry about that ole thing, lass. I know my niece took care of it. She always does. Clara takes good care of us all even as young as she is. Come, let's get in, out of the chilled night and into bed. Are you hungry?"

"Actually, yes, I am. How much for a bite?"

"Don't worry. It's on the house, missin' your bus and every-thing. You do like meat and cabbage?"

"Never had it but, I'll try it … smells delicious!"

"You just have a seat at the table in the other room and I will fix you a bowl."

Waiting wasn't long and she had a big bowl of soup (if that's what it was) and a hunk of homemade bread with butter in front of her. "Mmmm," Laura hummed, as she tasted the liquid.

"Eat up, baby. I will be in the kitchen if you need me." With those words, she left the room. Taking the spoon and eating the rest of the soup until the bowl was wiped dry with the bread, Laura couldn't remember the last time she ate a home-cooked meal. Getting up and bringing her dishes to the kitchen Laura couldn't believe, at this time of night, the woman was cooking and baking. The kitchen smelled like a four-star restaurant.

"Excuse me, I am done and it was great. I never had but will now! Your niece never told me your name."

"They call me Lizzie. It's short for Elizabeth, but I think it makes me sound old. Lizzie's fine, lass."

"Thank you again, Mrs. Lizzie. Can I go brush my teeth? Just point me and I should be able to find it." Lizzie looked up from the table she was kneading some kind of bread on. "Nonsense just let me wash up and I will get you there."

"Yes, ma'am."

Following up the stairs Laura couldn't help but notice the wall pictures. Just as the castle was earlier, they were everywhere. Some old and some new but every inch was covered. Showing her the bath and room, Lizzie excused herself and went back downstairs letting Laura to be. Glad she always had a toothbrush, she used the paste on the sink shelf and thought, *Lizzie wouldn't mind.* Cleaning up Laura headed toward her room. Closing the door and turning the light on, it was a pretty room with a double bed, dresser, nightstand, and lamp. Taking her clothes off, because she going to have to wear them again in the morning, Laura slipped under the covers with only panties on and fell asleep before turning out the light. A hard sleep is what she needed from the flight and the fresh air that she was not used to, but hard was not what she got.

Just as her body was into sleep, he was there, sitting on the bottom of the bed with one of her feet in his hands, rubbing it gently heel to her tiny toes. Then the other hand went up to her shins, rubbing them for a bit. It felt so good Laura just about melted right there. He didn't stop just kept going higher and higher until his fingers were at the ends of her legs and started on Laura's shoulders then the other, only stopping to place a soft kiss on her lips. Feeling a tug on her side as a slight push to roll onto her side, she turned. Curtis was sitting now on the side of the bed, rubbing her shoulders and back. Laura felt as if she was in dream heaven. Farther down her back the feeling went until Laura's body came alive as Curtis's fingers held her butt cheeks and rubbed. She knew that the female part was wet and wanting him to rub it also. He did not until his fingers completed. Now wanting more Laura felt a finger tracing the line between her cheeks, going over the spot that once was virgin but was no more. Down on to the center of her core, a soft sweep over the wet juices to repeat. Quickly a sweep became a penetration with one finger, then two into Laura's entrance. It almost sent her over the edge. With only two fingers inside, Laura felt every push and every knuckle on each.

As if this was not enough, a thumb came to rub the tiny flower bud above her entrance his fingers were in. Laura softly cried out.

Her muscles grabbed onto the fingers, the feeling of a steady pushing in and out as the body betrayed her mind. He didn't stop until she did. That's when he rolled her over and placed his mouth over her left breast and sucked as a hungry babe. Keeping his hand back where it had been only exiting to let Laura turn, his fingers were doing their magic again.

Alternating left and right on her breasts that now were wanting so much more, Laura thrusted her hips into the air and harder on his hand. Releasing his fingers from inside Curtis mounted while spreading the two thighs apart to allow his engorged penis to enter where his fingers were. Holding himself he put the head just into her lips, bent down, and covered her mouth with his, and when she opened for him, he filled her with all, pushing to the bottom, hip to hip, bones to bones. The harder the pushing, the harder the kisses, and the harder the pump into Laura became. With a moan from Laura's throat, he sped up, both releasing at the same time. Curtis slumped to one side and lay next to Laura. He whispered, "You are so close to where I rest, my love. I await you." Kissing his lips as to say, I am here, but when she did, he was gone, leaving just the lingering effects of their joining.

Shocked, Laura sat up, feeling disappointed and angry with her. "Am I crazy? Sex with only dreams. It is so real or mad?" Now very tired and angry, it was hard to fall back to sleep. She tossed and turned until she drifted off again, only to be awaken by a soft "good morning" calling from a female voice. It was Lizzie and she was waking her for breakfast. Sluggishly she gave a reply of "be right down." Lack of sleep was bad but lying in the night's sticky mess her body left topped it all. Another day has begun and Laura had things to do. Stomach growling, she got out of bed straight to the bathroom to clean, hoping no one else was in there. Dressed and awake, she opened the door. Her nose was accosted with the smells only a mother could make. Following, Laura went downstairs into the kitchen to see Lizzie right where she left her, only this time it wasn't dough but eggs and all the trimmings. "Morn. Want some eats for the day?" Lizzy asked with a smile.

"Yes, please. If it tastes like the soup last night, I might not want to leave."

Lizzie just laughed and shooed her out of the kitchen to wait for the plate. Coming out with a large plate of grub that was placed on the dining table, a cup of coffee already poured and a glass of orange juice if wanted, all set down and again a large welcoming smile.

"Enjoy." She left Laura to eat alone and time to think. The only thing that came to mind was "Does she ever sleep?" Cleaning up the plate and just about all on it, Laura waited for Lizzie to come back out, and when she did, the question came to mind but a funny gut feeling advised her not to speak of it and Laura normally listened so none was said. As Lizzie started to gather up the dishes, she let Laura know the bus would be coming soon, and that she might want to get ready.

"Okay, thanks." She headed upstairs to gather what little she brought. Coming down, she said a loud "thank you and thanks again," opening onto a very bright sun-shining day that about blinded her.

twenty-five

She covered her eyes as to squint until they had adjusted to daylight. Closing the door behind, Laura headed back to where the night started, the bar. Upon entering, the first face was Clara pouring a hot cup of coffee to the same guy (Liam) who was in the same seat of last night. She thought, *Does anyone go home and sleep in this town?* Shaking her head and accepting a cup of the hot stuff, Laura was asked if she had a restful night's sleep.

"Your aunt is really nice and she can cook wonderfully."

"Yeah, it's a wonder I don't weigh a bull's weight," Clara replied.

Taking a drink and now mustering to ask the question she didn't the night before, she asked, "Clara, do you know anyone by the name Cordley or of that line?"

Before she could even ask more, the man at the bar stopped in mid sip of drinking as if time froze him and everyone one else in earshot of the question. "Did I just go into the *Twilight Zone* movie?"

Clara turned and saw the mess she had made because as she heard the question she was spilling coffee everywhere. "Oh, shoot, look what I have done!" Clara didn't say anything. She just walked over to where Liam was sitting and looked directly at him. "Where is that name from? I have heard of it." He didn't answer in a long drawled breath.

Looking at Laura and saying in a sober and strong warning, he said, "You should go back where you came from and forget the name!" Standing with a why, Clara began to tell, "A long time ago, in a village just north of here, the family of Cordleys lived." She told that girls were told to scare them into coming in at night or walking alone day or night.

"Bullshit," Liam burst out. "Shshshs…you are gonna scare her!" Then he said, "The name you speak is that of a boy or man or demon! He is a vampire, cursed to it because he raped an old gypsy witch's granddaughter way back and set his life into the night."

Clara now yelled, "Lie, that's enough!"

Laura just sat there, grabbing her neck where she thought while making love (or dreaming of) he bit her. "This is a story, right? It's not true. Like you said, it was made up?" She asked with a worrying sound in her voice. "I don't know, but here in Ireland, there are all sorts of stories—banshees, leprechauns, demons, witches, etc." Liam again. "It's real, I tell ye! Real heard it since I was a wee lad. I, sis, and me da and his."

Laura then asked him what the name of the town was and he really didn't want to tell her but, she pleaded and he told her. "Lassie, ain't me ting but a town of rumbles now and everyone gone, moved away." Hearing the bus come up the road, she paid for the coffee with what bill she had and went out to meet it, now having a town name to go by.

Bus stopped and the driver saying a "good day" and let Laura on but told her he was going inside for some coffee and headed across the road with a thermos. Getting into a seat Laura found only a couple people who were fast asleep and wondering what they were dreaming of, if they were anything like hers. Finding was only fifteen minutes. Loading on and getting comfortable the bus was heading down the road the way it came. All the way back, Laura kept thinking of the story that was told to her, even though they said the name they knew as a creature, not the dream she knew.

Also the town's name gave her a starting place, now having to get more information before starting on the adventure. Looking down at her watch, it said 8:30 a.m. Thinking first thing was to get a map of this town Liam spoke about and go see Mrs. McPherson, to see what kind of info she had. Depending on that, Laura decided on renting a car if she could. Taking this, she didn't have to worry about schedules and could go where she wanted and when. Not to mention the reaction she got when asking questions and the reaction of people. She wasn't going to do that mistake again. The ride was shorter than on the way up (why does it feel like that?). The only difference was the amount of people that were out and about on the roadway in cars, trucks, and even horse-drawn carts. Now back in her hotel Laura stopped by the front desk just in case any messages were there, and yes, there was one from Mrs. McPherson. The note said someone cancelled, can she meet sooner. Was 1:00 p.m. good? Looking at the clock above the desk, it still gave four hours to five hours until one.

"Good." Laura then asked, "Where or is there any place to rent a car?" The clerk Joseph, by his name tag, said "Yes, one of the locals and he is pretty cheap." After writing down the number on a slip of paper, Laura went on up to her room to call. Hearing that there was a vehicle available and they would deliver, she said where she was and to leave the key at the desk and the desk clerk had all her payment information for the rental. To her shock they said okay and would leave the contract there for her to sign and to return it when the car was returned.

"Shower time," she said, heading for the bathroom. Getting a quickie because of time, Laura tried not to ponder on what happened, keeping in the back of her head as she dressed. Some parts crept up on her and she dismissed them fast.

Dressed and ready to go, Laura stopped, grabbed up the note pad by the phone, and wrote down her list she mentally made on the bus. "Already got the car. That's done!" Now get the map and go to her appointment at one.

Purse in hand then dropping it back onto the bed, she waited and waited. Her brain spoke to her being impatient, "Why isn't the car here yet?" Turning on the tube, she pushed the power button and *poof!* It came to life. At this time of day, it looked as if soap operas were the only thing on, so watching this foreign show, Laura got a good laugh. In the States, it's all who's sleeping with whom, or if it is not his baby, it's another etc. But here they didn't have any of that; here they have very busty redhead that wore low-cut shirts and some very handsome rugged-looking men. Yes, there were heated scenes but nothing like the States. Laura, tired of the PG-13, started to scan and found nothing when the phone beside her rung.

"Hello."

"Ms. Wilds, this is the front desk. Your car has arrived."

"Thank you. I'll be right down."

Turning the TV off, grabbing up all her necessities and the note she made for herself, she headed down.

When she got there the clerk handed the contract to her and Laura took a few minutes to read it before signing. Any damages or anything other than mechanical is the leaser's problem and will be fixed upon return of said vehicle. Laura signed and handed it back to the clerk who put it in the slot for her room. Going out to this car, Laura stopped short, forgetting in Ireland they drive on the other side of the road.

Smacking herself on the forehead because all the buses she'd been on in the past day she never paid attention. Now she would be driving, backward. She was going to give it a try. Going back into the lobby she asked the clerk quietly to use the parking area to practice, and with a polite smile (with a snicker) he said, "Yes, but try not to hit anything." Trying not to laugh, Laura too as it was funny. "Okay, fun time over." She sat in the driver seat, looking at the steering wheel, the gear shift, and the pedal. She eased the car forward, popping the clutch only once as she rode in the lot. Taking about a half hour to get used to this way of driving, Laura decided she was ready and aimed for the road. First gear she entered the roadway passing the inn and waiting for a car to pass that was going her way then scooted out behind it to keep herself on the right or wrong side of the road. As she drove and paid attention, Laura noticed even the road signs were different, but she could guess at the meanings (the colors were the same—yellow-yield, red-stop, green-go). Driving on no real direction or anywhere to be until one, which was still about an hour from now, she decided to ride and see what she could see.

As time passed she found herself out of town and up onto the farmlands where there were few people, cars, or anything modern. Hell, she even saw a woman getting water from a hand pump outside her home and thought, *What a simple life!* Now nearing a dead-end road, she pulled in and stopped, putting the car in first gear and applying the parking break. She sat wondering how she could have gotten here so fast. The road ended at what we would call a look-out area. Now she stepped out and did a 360 degrees, gazing at all that was in sight—vast landscapes that went on forever. She parked her butt on the hood of the car and let the view paint a mental photo in her mind that she could always revisit. Not realizing how long she sat, giving a gaze onto her watch, she was shocked that so much time had passed. She now had to head back for her appointment with Mrs. McPherson. "Damn, I could be here forever."

Heading back the way she came and slowly driving as she was still not accustomed to driving she went. Thinking as she drove, she began to think about staying in Ireland with its slow-paced way of life and people (from what she has met). "Don't judge one another." At that moment, his voice once again was in her head. "If you stay with me, we can live anywhere your heart desires. I will take care of you forever as you to me." Almost wrecking the car when he spoke to her, Laura really was getting angered because she never knew her brain talked back, and worse by a ghost she had yet to find. Only in dreams. Finally off the mountain and into town Laura tried to navigate the streets, having time because of the one-ways that were all over. She kept moving. Making left-hand turns when the road she wanted passed, she finally got to the street after doing another loop to go back she found the address and then there was another problem—parallel parking sitting ass backward in the driver's seat (left-hand driving). Passing she went a bit farther down and found a pull in parking that she could handle even though it was a half a block down. Ah, just a shrug of the shoulders and a "walk never hurt anyone!" Making it to the door within a good minute, she entered and Mrs. McPherson was sitting behind a desk typing away. Looking up, she said, "Hi, you must be Laura Wilds, I am presuming?"

"Yes, ma'am, I am sorry for my tardiness."

"I am still not accustomed to driving on the passenger side yet."

Mrs. McPherson laughed as she still typed and then stopped, grabbing the paper and placing it on her desk while she walked around to shake Laura's hand. "Well, I have some information. What I have might not help because, after the year 1783, the name Curtis Cordley vanished. It's nowhere on anything, not even a grave or death writing. Yet, I have good news too. There still are a few people with the name of Cordley."

Laura quickly asked, "What? You're kidding! The line still have family that are still alive?"

"Dearie, some of the families around here can trace their trees back to when people were fighting with wooden swords and crossing waters on boats they carved out of hollowed trees by hand." Now, Laura just couldn't believe what she was told but asked, "What do you think happened to Curtis. There has to be something?"

"Nope, if you go to the town where some of the last Cordleys live, they might be able to tell you."

"Okay, I will do that. Where is this town?"

Now a hesitant look came from the face of Mrs. Mc (as Laura now called her to herself).

"They say bad things have happened up there and none but the Cordleys that are left live there. It was, at one time, a very lively town they say. Now, lass, I am starting to frighten you. I don't mean to. The name is now called in stories Devil's Hill. There was another but it has been buried in the past."

Laura, looking frightened but intrigued, asked, "Is this place on any maps, and if not, how do I get there?"

"No, it is not on any. I can draw you directions, crude as they would be, if you like?" Grabbing a piece of paper Mrs. Mc. started to draw lines and land marks so Laura would not get lost. Finishing she handed the piece and told her that it was a good day's journey to get there and that it was way up in the hill so she should pack warmer clothes and be prepared to sleep in the car. There were no hotels or homes that were up there.

"Child, leave any emergency numbers before you leave as many have been said they go up but never come back!"

"Thank you for everything that you have done. How much do I owe you?"

Mrs. Mc just smacked her lips and said, "Nothing, I repaid a debt. Just come back. That's payment enough."

As Laura left she now felt very spooked out because with everything she has learned and the way Curtis came to her she really was beginning to think she was going nuts—just nuts enough to go and find out for herself. Walking back to the car and heading for the inn, she now had to get a coat that she didn't think she would need but, where would she buy one in summer? Remembering a clothing store she saw when driving the streets, she tried to recall the area where it was. On the way turning down one road and then another, she spotted it and, like a New York driver, cut into traffic into a parking stall, hearing honks as she cut cars off. Rushing out and into the store a cowbell alerted anyone working of the door opening and someone entering. From somewhere in the back, a large corn feed (as we say in the States) looking woman appeared. "Can I help you?"

"Yes, I need a warm coat to wear."

"Over there." The woman pointed to the far wall area. Let me know if you need any more help."

"Okay," Laura replied. Walking over she couldn't get the feeling of being in one of the stores back home. They were very similar. Rummaging through the pile and finding one that had a hood and lots of pockets, she got the attention of the woman and asked how much, then if she took credit cards. The woman nodded, and walking up to the front, Laura stopped because she noticed a really cool-looking sweater and thought Jamie would like to have it, so picking it up along with the coat and paying, she left.

"One down and food to go, plus a good blanket just case." These she would buy at a retail store. "As Mrs. Mc said I might have to sleep in the car." Heading back to the inn, a thought of sending the sweater express to Jamie came. Parking the car at the inn and heading to the desk she asked if there was mailing through it. The answer was yes, so she gave the mailing info for the label and then was asked if a box or bag was needed. "Yes, thank you." Now that was done and paid for on the tab of the room of course, she headed back up to her room for a good night's sleep before heading into BFE. Entering, the TV was turned on and clothes started to come off as she walked into the shower thinking about what Mrs. Mc said. With no places to stay, she was going to get a good wash before the new day. Dipping one foot into the water (as a shower was too quick for her), she slid the rest of her leg and body down into the water till every part of her was covered except her neck up. Laying her head back and laying a towel under it Laura closed her eyes to relax. When she closed them, a cool, crisp flow of the air conditioner came to her. Before she knew it, the combination of hot water and being in cool air had her fast asleep in the tub. Unknown how long she had dozed off, it was long enough for the water to become cold. She woke, pulling the plug and letting the water out, standing up, drying off she stepped into the room. Wrapping a towel around her more out of habit, she headed straight for the covers and into bed, dropping the towel onto the floor. Laying there between the sheets, her mind raced with possibilities of what she was going to find. How would the people treat her when showing up on their doorsteps (if they even had some)? Would they turn her away or welcome her? Falling asleep, this time thinking of Curtis.

Within only about an hour or so of falling into the blackness of sleep, he entered into her world of slumber and thought what she was thinking. Sitting on the edge of the bed and wondering what a life would be having her in his life for eternity, then taking a slight movement of Laura's legs as he pulled up the covers and slipped under them just wanting to feel her warmth next to him. He didn't want to do anything with her tonight unless Laura herself willed it. They lay together, she asleep and he watching her sleep. Laura turned again, this time face-to-face. He still just watched, and slowly and beautifully, Laura opened her eyes to look into his, when she very quietly whispered, "You came. I was just thinking of you before I fell asleep."

"I know as I was you, my love."

When his sentence was cut short with the glorious feeling of her lips upon his, the just lying there became something more. Entwining into each other and asking if she was sure, he undressed and lay back down skin to skin, and then each began to travel and explore one another as they held the opposite hand of each above their heads. Her hand was the first to hold and begin to stroke him up and down till his erection was strong and stiff. Then his hand next found her already moist and ready for him to enter, whether it was his fingers or another part of him. He entered her slowly because he loved the way his fingers slid into her. The walls of her womanhood would clutch around them and hold on. Pushing in and out, not fully all the way, he could feel her building into the first climax of the evening and he maintained this rhythm until her legs squished his hand and he could feel the pulsing. Holding his fingers inside her until she completed, he opened her thighs, placing one thigh onto his hips and moving his body closer to hers. He placed the head of his shaft inside Laura about only an inch as he kissed her now-swollen lips. A breath as he entered with only a hard and extended push, a moan came from her throat as she felt him enter her all the way. Just as slow and hard as he went in, he came back out only to repeat this motion many times more. Feeling her grabbing onto him he knew she was ready for another and he quickened the strokes, each time hitting the end of her canal until he could not hold himself any longer and, within a few more thrusts harder hitting that spot, they both let themselves go, her milking him and him releasing his seed with each pulse.

Now fully and completely sleepy, Laura fell asleep within his arms, him still inside her. He too closed his eyes as he held her to sleep. This time was different because Laura woke to find him still lying beside her and she snuggled in his chest with soft kisses and softly said, "I will be looking for you today." When he woke, he gently placed his hand under her chin, bringing her mouth up to his for a lovely, sensuous kiss that made each of their bodies come back to life and they made love twice more before Laura felt the urge to pee. She started to roll and stopped because his words drifted. "I am waiting" as he let go. Waking in a pre-sitting way she went to the bathroom, enlightened from the passion of the night only to return to an empty bed. There was no sign of him anywhere and the door was still locked. Already thinking she's going crazy, she chalked this dream again to the stages of madness.

Glancing up at the clock after and sitting on the bed, it was already 5:30 a.m. And her alarm set for six. There was no need. Shutting it off and starting to get another shower, which she felt was a déjà vu, she freshened up from the night's mess. As she washed her thoughts went to the days to come and the answers she hoped for.

CHAPTER

twenty-six

Dressed and gathering all her stuff she had brought because why pay for a room if you're not going to stay, Laura walked down to the elevator to the front desk and checked out. Waking the clerk, she signed the bill and left a note with the information on it that Mrs. Mc said to leave. She handed the clerk with instructions: "If I am not back in a week, open this and call the numbers. Report me as missing, please."

The clerk, with a puzzled look, said, "Okay."

Going straight to the only store that was open at this time, she bought some food and drinks enough to last at least a week plus extras—flashlight (with extra batteries), matches (waterproof), a lighter, and the ole never forget a hand-crank can opener (no power-DAH), and seeing they had some throw blankets, she got a few of them too (can never have enough covers). Oh, and she almost forgot the map. She paid and with an arm full of stuff she headed to the car. She placed everything in the backseat so she had room to drive and spread out the map and left to head for the hills.

This road that she was on was nothing like the bus tour. In fact, it was more surreal, taking her up where the forest meets the sky. Still the countryside was just as pretty as another except, the farther she drove, the more it started looking like a horror movie. With its tall trees, trees together, trees apart, and in some none at all but a sloping side of rock with green grass where (in her mind was where murder happens) but no trees. Even with a vivid imagination, Laura kept climbing. Hours had passed and not a soul, not even a shack, nothing. It was well into the late morning hours when her body decided time to stop. Pulling over, she got out, opened the back of the car to find the toilet paper, then walked off into the shrubs. Even though there was no one in sight, it still was something women do (hide to pee). Wiping and covering the puddle and paper with dirt, she went back to the car, stretched, and just looked around. "Wow, you don't see this in the States. No one around, not even a sound of airplanes!"

Taking about thirty minutes just to bring in the site, she huffed as she sat back into the car to head on. Driving and driving was really a boring way to travel by one's self, she thought, reaching to turn on the radio, which didn't get much reception. She began to sing (why not no one here to hear). Time passed slowly but she looked at her watch and it was already past three in the afternoon. She thought she'd drive until she was tired or something happened. Again she looked at the watch as the sun was going down and she had to turn the head lights on as the road was getting harder to see from the darkness. Driving another half hour, she found a nice spot, open and with a full view of anyone approaching. She got out, gathered up a blanket, toilet paper (just in case) using the seat as a bed, and the door for a pillow, rolling down the windows for ventilation she lay down and opened her book to read.

Didn't take long before the reading and the traveling set her to dream world. This night she slept alone. All alone in the open, in a car, on a mountain with a cell that didn't work and not even a farmhouse she could see. Waking with a startle to a tapping on the window, there was a large man with an even bigger beard, white in color as if he took snow and placed it on his face. He stood there just a tapping. "Lassie, lassie, are you okay?" he spoke in a very thick accent. She rolled the window down a bit more and told him she was fine, that she was heading to one of the towns up farther on the mountain. He asked where. He swooshed a sheep from getting around the car—yep there were actually people who still walked with their livestock just like in books. When she told him where she was going, his face turned from a caring sheep farmer to a concerned and very stern man, telling her she need not go there that it was an evil place where demons lived. But when asked why it was so evil, he just shook his head and kept saying, "Evil, evil place!" He didn't talk to her no more. He just walked off, him and his sheep.

Laura, now fully awake and the sun just rising over the top of the mountain, unkinked her legs and got out of the car only to find mornings up here were very cold, so thankful to Mrs. Mc for the advice and to herself, she grabbed the coat and put it on quickly. With no bathroom but having some wet ones she always carried in her purse, she washed her face, better than nothing, she thought. Not knowing where the sheep man was, she waited to go to relieve herself.

Starting the engine and allowing it to warm up, taking a few look over the map again, she noticed there was a turn she had to take to the left at a sign Mrs. Mc couldn't recall what it read only that it was between two really big rocks.

Knowing she hadn't passed anything like that yet, she knew she was still on the right road. How much farther was anyone's guess. She put the car into D and headed forward up the road and up and up. The road felt like it was never going to level out, yet she drove. Floating now as to not using the bathroom, her teeth felt like they were. She stopped to relieve the tiny bag in her body known as the bladder and humped an "ahahhahah." Finished and cleaned up, she drove again, still not seeing anything but up and feeling as if it was never going to end. There in the foreground sat what looked like a wall, but they were the rocks, and yes, they were very large, as a truck. Sitting idle she looked around to see the path or dirt roadway in which she was told to take. Turning just a bit she started to head down only the feeling as she drove went from warm countryside to looking over her shoulders. She was not happy with it but went on.

This road at times looked as if it would disappear then come back enough for her to know she was still on it and drivable. Thinking no one must have driven (in vehicles) very often maybe that's why it looked as it did, and this made her feel a bit safer. Coming to a large tree in the road and seeing a split in the lane, she couldn't remember which way she was to go so retrieving the map, it showed that the left was her route and proceeded to go in the direction. Now this was again taking her up until she realized the top of the mountain was just ahead. She drove to the crest, stopping just to gaze over the dash at the never-ending scene that lay before her. "Damn, how many people she knew has ever gotten to see a land so big and untouched from modern life?"

Breathtaking was the thought rolling in her head as she drove along this narrow road sitting among the sky where gods could only touch. She snapped back to reality and headed down till the road tapered off into a tree line, thankful for the day's light because at night it could resemble the story of Little Red Riding Hood and the Wolf. Into the wooded canopy she went. Out of nowhere a deer ran in front of the car and almost became car breakfast, then a dog and another and another. Almost not believing what she was seeing, she blinked with a jump into the back of her seat. To what looked like teenage boys running tight behind the dogs, they were chasing the deer. She saw them, and when they saw her and the car, they froze right where their feet landed. The look on each of the boy's faces was pure fright! Like they had never before accepted anyone to be there in these woods but them. After a few tense moments, the taller boy walked over to the car where Laura was sitting freaked out (the younger child didn't move).

In a very Irish hills drawl, he said, "Lady, is you lost 'cause ye be a long way from any town."

Almost laughing because of the way he spoke and what he said, Laura held herself in check and asked if he knew where this place was, pointing to the map she held out for him to see. His eyes got big as he looked and asked, "Why she wanted to go there?"

Telling him the cliff notes version, he surprised her by telling her not only how to get directly there but that he lived there with his little brother he called Ivan and he Christoph. To make her brain fry even more, he gave directions to his home, and if she waited down the path, they would introduce her to the rest of their family. Laura agreed and traveled back down through the woods to the area the boys said and waited. While she waited the warnings that were told to her seemed unwanted because, so far, even though they were boys, these kids didn't seem like they would eat her and make necklaces out of her bones. Sitting, waiting for what seemed like a half hour, there was a rap on the window. There they were with the carcass of the deer they were chasing. Laura asked them where the dogs were because she only saw one and they told her that they had sent the others home and Dude always stayed with them, which thinking back, he was with them when they talked earlier. Moving things around and letting the boys into the car, she helped and watched as Ivan slung the deer onto the hood of the car and held it by its legs. She asked if there would be any blood and the boys laughed.

"Naw, we drained the blood 'cause it's not good to have it run all down one's back when carrying the meat home."

She just laughed in return. "Well, that makes sense." All three just laughed together. Traveling down the road, she asked Christoph (who seemed more apt to talk than his brother) about some of the stories she was told and he politely, almost jokingly, said that most of them weren't true. It was just stories that got told over and over. As they went on, they got bigger. Laura did ask him if his parents would be angry when they arrived for bringing a stranger home.

Ivan perked up, "Nay, me mamma she be a very welcoming woman."

She thought that was such a cute way to say mom coming from such a little guy. Christoph pointed and showed where to turn and said their home was around the turn in the road. Not long and rounding the turn, Laura could not believe the landscape of these boys' home. "You two live here? It's really pretty!"

The two of them in harmony say, "Aye."

Seeing a vehicle come down the road, there stood the boys da (in English, that's dad). He was in the paddock and came out to see who was coming to his home, with a deer lying on the hood. Even before the car stopped, Ivan jumped out and ran over to him telling something, but was soon to find out. "My boy Ivan sais here that you gave them a ride with the meat and that you are a nice lassie. I am their da. Imas McLouluny and you have met me boys."

"Laura Wilds, sir, glad to meet ya. You have two very good boys here who, by the looks, I have seen hunt very well also."

"Aye, that they do, lass, that they do! Ivan, run up and gather yer ma," his dad said and without hesitation he was off. All heard was

"Ma, Ma, there's a nice lassie here" and more she couldn't understand. Standing there Christop grabbed up the deer and went off into the barn. Laura guessed to skin it out or something. She and the father and had made small talk as they waited for his wife to join them. When she did, Laura noticed she was a middle-aged woman with lines on her face, not of worry but a hard life and that she was pregnant. She looked to be six to eight months pregnant. Introductions were made and Inga, as her husband called her, said, "It's cool out here and this bucket so heavy. Let's get inside. Where's Christop?"

"He's in the barn with a deer," Imams said as they walked into the house.

Entering, Laura liked what she saw. By the outside it looked like a shambles, but inside, it was like a well-built home in any town in the States and Laura said to Inga, "Your home is very pretty!"

Blushing, Inga replied, "All thanks be to my husband. He put hard work into making our wee house a castle."

After taking off their coats and hanging them up, they all sat down in what looked like the living area surrounding a large fireplace that kept the whole place warm. Inga came into the room with a tray of beverages and cheese with bread.

"Please help yourself," Imas stated.

Being a bit on the hungry side and defiantly thirsty Laura only took a few pieces as not to look like a pig. Inga asked with a questionable face what a woman would be traveling all alone and being a foreigner, why she was? Laura then started to explain the detective's story about the fingerprints and how strange it was. Laura also added that they pretty much closed the case, yet she herself had not and then she went on to add about the letters. Both Imas and Inga sat listening not looking like they were making any judgments until the way their faces changed at the name Curtis Cordley. Then came the questions or the questions with the warnings Imas who was quick to state and bluntly, "Lass, that is a name we in these woods speak none of. Their name and family have been gone for many years, except the last of thee line and they are almost dead themselves." Inga who sat very quiet because of the look she was given by her husband but she also had a look like she also knew the stories but did not believe them yet she said nothing. Laura then asked him why. "Why are people so afraid of this family? Even the townspeople below cringed from the very hearing of it." She then added that she was told a story and asked if she could repeat it to conclude its truth.

He shook his head but said, "Aye, I will listen to agree or deny." So she repeated what Clara had told her and how the man sitting at the bar reacted. He sat and listened till the story was ended and agreed to it without adding anything to or from only that it was getting late and morning comes early. But he did invite her to stay on the condition there would be nay more talk of the Cordley name in his home. Laura agreed and thanked him as Inga was getting up to show her the room she would be sleeping. Following her down the small hall to a room that when the door was open looked like one of the boy's rooms, Laura asked, "Your son won't mind?" With a nod and "O'Lordie, no. Most of the time he is asleep out by the fire in a chair. Done worry ye head."

"Oh." Laura just shyly replied. "Thank you again."

Inga explained where the bathroom was if she needed to freshen up and also asked if she needed any bed clothes as to her sister some days stays and is her size so she could borrow a gown. Laura politely refused and just said she would sleep in her clothes. With that Inga left closing the door behind her. Looking around she thought to herself that this family might live way out up in the hills but their children were very modern boys with the posters of girls and rock bands and surfing photos/posters on every wall. Laura laughed because one would have thought otherwise by the outside appearance of their home. "Never judge a book by its cover!" she said.

Taking off her shoes and unbuttoning her jeans (they do get tighter if you sleep in them), she got under the covers that she found to be heavily made and by hand by the feel of them. It didn't take long for her to fall asleep even in a stranger's bed and all. This night didn't have any visitors but it did have strange images as woods, water, dark places that Laura thought were caves and people that she never seen before. Not a dream, or was it a nightmare? It was just images in her head as she slept One was of a younger female and a figure behind her holding her head and what looked like he was kissing her neck, or was it something other than a kiss? Laura awoke, finding she was holding her own neck in the area of the two long gone marks.

"I don't know which is worse, waking with the thought of being bitten or having wild and crazy sex with a ghost?" Laura said to herself as she was waking up. Yawning and getting her nose filled with the smell of something really tasty she swung her feet over the bed, put on her shoes, fastened the button on her jeans, and tried to remember where the bathroom was. Opening the door and now really being able to smell it and not having to look for the bathroom because the youngest boy, Ivan, was coming out and she asked, "Bathroom?" He just nodded and went back into a room she assumed was his. Closing the door and just doing the splash piss-and-dry method, she exited and headed into the center of part of the home where Inga was in the kitchen and gestured for her to come. Then she offered Laura a large plate of bacon, eggs, toast, and something that looked like grits or porridge (she couldn't tell), and then sat down with her after making a plate for herself.

"I waited for you to rise and we or I could have someone to eat with that's not a man!" She laughed while she said it. They both giggled and Inga then asked about town and some of the places that she knew of. Laura really couldn't answer her but she tried from what she saw on her ventures of the tours. Inga told her that it had almost been six months since any of them had went anywhere. They only go for the staple products and some household items that cannot be hunted or made here at home. She wasn't complaining but was just curious. Her sister sometimes takes her away, but Imas really doesn't like it, yet he lets her go anyways. They finished eating and Laura helped clean up even though Inga said she didn't need it but was grateful anyways.

Now she let Laura know that she had to go on with her chores and that she had made a basket for her to take with her on her journey. Smiling and with a thank you, they both grabbed their coats and walked outside. Before letting Laura go, Inga did ask if she would stop back by. Though Laura was a stranger, she liked her and welcomed the company. "Sure, after I find what I am looking for, thanks again." They hugged, and basket in hand, Laura got into her car.

Turning the engine and letting it warm, she was back to whatever "it" was to find. About a mile or so down the road and smelling the basket Inga had given her, she couldn't stand it any longer. The smell was just too great. Pulling the cloth back Laura saw rolls, slices of cheese, a couple of small containers of drinks, and a piece of paper tucked between the drinks. "What the...?" She took it out to read.

Imas would not let me tell you there is an old woman and younger boy up on the mountain that have the last name you spoke of. People do not go to them nor do they come down. Be wary!

And there was a map drawn from the road ending where you turn from the home. Laura couldn't believe what she read or what luck she had been given, but she looked at this map and the one that Mrs. Mc had drawn and the only difference was a couple of turns. Instead of the town, it was to a house. She was driving in the right direction but still had half day's drive ahead of her though.

Finally getting to where the maps differed, Laura decided to venture into the abandoned town first since it was daylight. Some twenty minutes or about and she started to see signs of some kind of place, road signs (wooden and old) knocked over on the ground, pieces of wood, and old fallen down shells what maybe could have been homes or even shops on the road way. Now they were just piles of rubble and nothing to be sought, so she went on until the road ended, not in the way of an old road would but with a pile of dirt and trees that was put there as to keep people out or something in. Getting out and putting her coat back on, she walked up to the blockage when, kicking rocks and things on the ground, she noticed a flat piece of board and picked it up. To her horror some of it could still be read:

Beware Do Not Enter D**** @*@*@*

The rest she could not read and some of those words were not there but she pieced them like a puzzle. "Holy shit! These people weren't fooling around. They were really scared of this town!" But Laura being Laura and wanting answers, she decided, since she couldn't drive, obviously she would walk. Going back to the car and getting a flashlight, blanket (just in case), her wallet, and the basket Inga made (it was too good to leave for someone else to eat if they broke into her car), she started walking out so having plenty of time to explore before sun down. She clambered over the pile and down the other side, stopping abruptly at what she was seeing. It looked like a set out of a horror movie, complete with dirt road, two sides of a street with buildings (crumbling in places but still standing) that still had signs that hung outside and what really got her was, in the mud road, there were prints where someone had been here, recently. Getting a bad case of the goose bumps but still not freaked enough, she ventured, more curious. Walking on the road so she could see both sides her head and eyes switched from left to right and back again, just absorbing this sight no one in many, many years have seen. "Oh my, this looks like it was a very busy place at one time," she spoke out loud to herself. Going closer now to the buildings on the left and peering into the windows that had no glass left in some of them, she saw tables, chairs, and even cups and bowls still right where they were left. Not going in, she still just did the window-shopping effect, looking. Every opening she could see into, she looked until next to the last little window when there were still pictures on the walls, the only way in was entering carefully because through one of the windows, and as old as these buildings were, she didn't want anything falling on her head, pushing on and on gently and getting an opening just big enough for her to squeeze.

CHAPTER
twenty-seven

Entering, the first thing was the amount of dust or dirt that covered most of the furniture, chairs, tables, and counter. Slowly, she ventured farther in, and when she got close enough to see the pictures, she saw not photos as we know today but painted pictures with very life-like people in them. Thinking someone was very talented to be able to create such works, Laura was just wowed by the details. Looking at each there were some with very important-looking people like a mayor or town sheriff (if that's what they were called then). Some others were family portraits—fathers, mothers with children and some that were damaged to which the colors and pictures could not be made out. None really caught her attention, yet they were neat just to look at. Going out the same way she came in, she went across the road to the other windows and stores to gander what she could see while the sun was still up. Most on this side were just empty shacks. Doing a walk by, the next windows contained a cage, in the back of the open room. *I wonder if this was the jail,* she thought, now seeing that the door looked as if it was a jar she tried, and yep, it would open without coming down around so she went in. Even though the window had no glass, it didn't look safe. As soon as she was in, a burst of wind came and sent a cloud of dirt mixed with dust all over her and the room as if it came to life when she entered. Choking she stopped and let the wind pass, waving her hands in front of her face to try and keep from breathing too much in. As all the cloud started to drop back down to the floor, she thought she was seeing a shape of someone standing there in there in the cell that was closed and very dingy in the corner. Shocked, Laura held her breath until she could see that no one was there, it was only her imagination and a lot of dust. "Damn, that creeped me out!"

Now she stood there keeping a watchful eye on the cell over her shoulder. Walking over to the small desk that sat in the room, she opened a few drawers to nothing but dust. Still more to open she continued, nothing until the last one. Grabbing the handle and giving a pull, a thud was heard, then she pulled a little harder and popped the drawer open, but she didn't see anything. She bent down so she could reach in as far as she could and felt a hard, long object. She slowly pulled it out. As she brought it out with her hand, grasping it, she felt a sting. "Ouch, what the!" As she pulled it out she saw a darkened reddish-colored line on the inside of her palm. Right where now to see was a blade from a bone-handled knife. With the other hand Laura reached into her pack and took out a rag, then started to wrap her hand, which was now bleeding. Having the hand covered she went to a space where the light was better to see this knife, which was quickly dropped onto the floor because seeing her blood on the blade shocked her. Picking it back up and now back to her senses, she looked more closely. But what got her attention was not her blood but the stain that was below; there under hers was a darker older color that looked like blood. "Oh great, I just gave myself some sort of blood poison in the middle of nowhere!" Not that she was thinking but when looking at this weapon more, she noticed, when turning the handle in her hand, was the initials of CM. They were carved deep into the bone handle. Laura just stood there staring until a gust of wind came through the opened doorway. *Oh dang, that all I need a storm.* Double-checking the wrap on her hand and tossing the knife into her pack, she headed out of the door and into the road. Looking down and seeing that her hand was bleeding through the wrap she headed back to the car for more medical supplies and some shelter from the storm. Making a good go at it was good, but she was not fast enough because as she was walking sometimes backward to keep the sting of the dirt from beating her skin to death, Laura didn't figure this storm to be so fast and strong when a tree limb came from nowhere, landing right in front of her, making a stumble of footing and making her trip. Falling with a twist, she went down hard. Ass, back head, and feet into the air, and when her body hit the ground, all that was said was UGH because she hit the branch right the center of her back and head. This is when the lights went out. She never made it back to the truck.

She lay in the road of an abandoned town with an open cut on her hand and no one really knowing where she was. Waking by the strange sensation of someone shaking her, Laura's eyes were still foggy but opened to see a very scary-looking old woman who, when she spoke, had no teeth in her mouth and was wearing what look like a rag's pile. "Missy, are you okay? Miss, what are you doing here all by yourself?" It was really hard to hear her from the wind and roar of the storm. "O' my you are a young lass. You need to get up. Come follow. I shall take you to my cabin. It's not far but we must hurry before it gets too dark." Trying to get up herself, Laura didn't do very well and the woman, placing her arm under Laura's, helped, then kept it there to help balance Laura up. The fall must have given her a slight concussion. Her balance, vision, and coordination were way off and she had a raging headache. Oh, let's not forget the throbbing coming from her hand. The strange woman kept Laura moving and muttering something like "Must hurry before dark, must hurry before dark, hurry." As the dusk steeled into dark, the woman quickened the pace and muttered on and on more now. Laura felt as though it took hours but was only twenty minutes and she was inside a small-framed very old cabin. Getting in and the ole woman laying Laura down, her head went to swimming and she was out, back into darkness. The old woman cleaned and bandaged Laura's wounds that were very deep, the both of them. She had to put stitches in the one on her head, but Laura didn't feel anything.

Three days come and gone before Laura woke and could see where she was. Still had a headache, but at least her eyesight was back. Sitting up and hearing movement in the smaller room that was attached to the room she lay, Laura tried to get up but lost her balance and fell onto a wooden floor with a thud. The old woman came running or walking fast as she could be heard saying, "No, no.

You are still too weak to start moving around, take one step at a time, child."

Laura looked up at the woman and asked who she was as she helped her back into the oversized sofa/bed. Once the woman got her back down and in a propped up position, all tucked in again, she sat in the chair and took a deep breath as she looked directly at Laura. "Child, I nay know if ye would ever come back to the living. You were for many days with fever and lost between worlds. I am Salina MacValski, but you may just call me Salina. I mended your wounds and kept the poison from grasping your life. You have a wee nasty cut on you hand that became very angry with infection. The head wound was just a couple stitch and done, but the bump gave ye brain a real wonder through the between lands. May know if yer would come back. Yet here ye are looking strong enough to fight ye demons."

Laura reached up to her head and felt in her hair where there were two very fine pieces of twine sewed into her skin. "They can come out in another few days or so. Don't worry, child. No one will even see a scar up in your pretty hair."

"Thank you, Salina, for helping me, but what do you mean by the between lands and demons?"

Salina took a sip of her hot drink that was in her well-drank-from cup and said, "O, child, you were speaking to a many folks when ye were in fever."

"Like who?" Laura asked, wide-eyed, afraid Curtis had come to her. She couldn't remember this time. Saline began with "You called for your mother many times mostly asking why she never told you something and how she could leave you alone so soon. At one time you hollered for grandma, only once and most of it was gibberish. I could not understand, and you did call for a man, named Curtis. Is he your husband?" Laura looked shocked as Salina told her that she called for him.

"No, he is not my husband. He is…" And she stopped.

"Now, Laura, you have no need to be shy. I am an old woman and lived many, many years. You can tell."

"I don't even know if he's real," Laura said. "You will probably think of me as crazy!"

"No, you seem to have your senses about you, only God knows why you are alone in this cursed place but go on."

Feeling very safe with her she started to tell the story, Salina sitting quietly and without judgment until Laura said his name. At this time she raised an eyebrow and now had a strange twinkle in her eyes and still said nothing.

As Laura went on she told the whole story without leaving anything, except certain parts but for some reason she felt as if Salina already knew of those. Ending the story and feeling the headache coming back down, Laura sat back down and Salina gave her a drink that would help with the pain and let her sleep. As Laura lay sleeping, Salina searched through some of her things, looking for a book that was handed down in her family for generations. When she found it and unwrapped it from its protective cover, she placed her hands over it, and in a language of her ancestors spoke, "Va Ti Kromby Vi Nonte," which translated into "It's time to end this."

With a sigh, she went back to her chair and waited for Laura to wake again so she could tell her the story of her reasons to still be walking this plane of the living and their destiny that was intertwined many years past.

This time as she slept, she saw many things, people that were not of this time. She was seeing through someone else's eyes and their life or wasted lives Laura could not be sure. But what she did come to understand while sleeping was that Curtis was her past, present, and future. Yet so was Salina. As she slept, her mind was piecing a puzzle together for her to complete. Opening her eyes this time to sunshine and Salina sitting in the same spot. Laura stared at her and said only four small words: "You and I are..." She was stopped by a finger to Salina's lips and just nodded her head as if she understood.

Now looking at Laura, Salina began, "What I am going to speak you must have your mind open because we are all on a path of the unknown until we venture or as you have stumbled upon it." As she spoke she opened the book.

Laura seeing this old book asked, "What is that?"

Salina, still opening and turning to the first page, said, "This is our destiny! Come closer so you may see the pages more clearly, child." Sitting now Laura felt as if she was a small child getting ready for a bedtime story starting with the first page.

"My family from the beginning. My grandmother many generations back was a gyspy as was her daughter and so on, just as I am today." Flipping pages she told of the hardships of living the gypsy life and the wonderful powers that come from practice and belief. Then there on the pages that were just turned were words to picture, the picture Laura could interrupt but the words forget it. What she saw was a wagon and a girl and the name Curtis Cordley. Eyes wide now, Salina went on to tell the story as was told to her. Still turning pages and speaking, she stopped only briefly and turned to say, "This is where our lives meet or shall I say our ancestors foretold."

Now looking very curious Laura just waited as Salina went, "On your family, at least from the female side, came here to the mountain. They were a small bunch with very few men so your grandmother's grandmother's grandmother and her husband sold her to a pioneer that was seeking a bride. They sold her because she was not pure of her maiden head because of a man named Curtis McCordley and his wrongful ways. No, they did not get much for her but the man took her anyways only to sell so she was not sold to someone else. You see, he lied about needing a wife as he did not need one. And could not see this woman sold like a dog, he took your ancestor and went off over the seas to what is now the Americas. Then my great, great, great-grandmother, before her death, spoke of the curse that was set in place and handed my mother this book and was told to keep it until the time would come for the curse to be broken."

Now Laura, fully not understanding anything, spoke up, "Am I to believe the curse. Is that why all this has been happening to me? Why my mother didn't tell me? Your mother and grandmother were not strong enough. They fell in love with a spirit and could not do what has to be done. But let me finish, please! The curse can only be broken by the daughter that will see the spirit if what he is not what he was even though she has felt the passion he can give. You, Laura Wilds, are that daughter that. That is why you have come here, leaving all who you have known behind and not knowing where you will go."

"Salina, I am not as strong as you think. I am not the daughter to which you speak!"

Turning another page of the book, there was a picture that Laura looked at and stared at, for there on paper was an image that looked like her. Smiling now Salina just softly said, "Child, you have been waited on for many years. Only you can stop this and make things right as they should be!

"You and I must prepare for this now. Get some rest. We shall start at the sun's rising." Getting slowly up and unbending her legs that were now pretty stuck in their position heading to the bed she had been laying in, Laura slid under the sheets and slowly relaxed as a headache again was coming on. Salina had also got up and headed into the kitchen, guessing what she would needed for the morning. Before Salina returned, Laura was asleep. Looking at her and smiling, she sat back into her chair reaching over and into a basket to retrieve her yarn and needles. As Laura slept her mind was wide awake with thoughts from family, her mom and grandma especially with the question of "why." After her mind tried to sort out the reasoning to no avail, she finally fell off into the dreaming stage and this was where he waited. Only, instead of being in her bed, they were back on the cliff overlooking the blue green waters of the cove they first met at or she dreamed. As the wind blew and their bodies are laying upon the other, Laura looked up into his face, the face she once thought of as an angel. But now looking there was another, and this faces cared her.

Curtis, feeling this difference in her touch and in her eyes, questioned it, "Laura, why do you fear me now after all the intimacy we have done? Do you not trust me as you had? I love you and would never hurt a hair on your body..." Not being able to complete his sentence because her finger was gently lying over his lips.

She spoke softly, "Why could you not have trusted me with happened to you? I have come all this way to find you and make the fairy tale you have created come true. Instead, I find truth of things that you have done and why you are who you have become."

He kissed her with such passion and force that her breath was halted and there was no more words spoken.

When this kiss ended, Laura's body was on fire. For him and for her no words were now needed. As passion took the both of them over and beyond the realms of the world he had them in. Then everything stopped when a voice they both heard between each moan said, "Laura, you must not allow this to continue. He needs to be set free!" Curtis, taking his mouth away from Laura's breast, looked over her body to see an old woman standing there looking at the two of them.

"Woman, how do you dare to interrupt me!" Curtis yelled very angrily. "You have no right to interfere with my doings!"

"Nay, Curtis McCordley, I have every right as was passed down to me in blood, a blood that you stole and started this journey with," Salina snapped back showing no fear. The whole time Curtis and Salina were speaking Laura could hear them but could do nothing but have the feeling she needed to have him with his fingers. As he was doing with a vengeance. As she had his swollen shaft in her hands and stroking it with all its length, wanting more Laura moved under him, placing the head just outside her moistened opening. With his finger still inserted it deeply inside and she, along with his finger, glided the length of him passed the folds and along his finger into her with a push of her hips. This was all done with Salina watching and Curtis watching her. He did not care as he thought to himself, *One old woman has no powers with or over thee!*

Now he was moving in and out of Laura like he was riding a stallion in full gallop as she thrusted up to him. Her hips pushed up and back down to allow his shaft more entrance. Faster, harder, and deeper with every movement until he felt the synching and pulsing of Laura's muscles, milking him with every push. Entering now to the hilt of his balls and feeling the end of her moist cave to where only babes exist, he looked at Salina and a few more movements of his hips, he bent down to Laura's ears and whispered, "Soon, my love, it shall be forever!"

Salina stood there until he was gone and then she was. Only Laura was left behind. After returning to her body sitting in the chair, Salina then got up and walked over to Laura to wake her. Nudging her shoulders and softly saying, "Child, wake now. We must begin." Having to repeat this because Laura was in such a sleep and compiled with feelings of desire she opened her eyes. Then the questions and more of embarrassment of knowing she saw them together.

"Oh my! Shit, Salina, you were there standing, watching us—me, us doing! Why or how did you do that?"

Now sitting back into her chair Salina sipped on her cup and in her own time replied, "I needed to follow him back to where his body lays. No one has ever known after his departure where he's hidden. Now because of you, it can all be finished."

"But you watched us have sex and did nothing yet watch!"

"If I had intervened, he would have known what I was doing and up boundaries as so I could not follow but as he was in the moment and thinking he was superior, he was not threatened, just wanted to make a show. As once he knew I was there, he never took his eyes off me as a challenge." Wide eyes and now very embarrassed Laura chokingly asked, "Do you know where this place is? I have been there twice with him."

"Yes, child, I do believe I do, and you should not be embarrassed as I was young once too, although many years ago, and do remember what it is like to make love so patiently, but you have forgotten or almost that he is a monster. He has brought on himself!"

Shouting now, Laura says, "He's not a monster!"

"Maybe not to you but his punishment has made it so," Salina rebutted.

Laura had only one question left. "What will happen to him when we do this? Is he going to die?"

Shaking her head Salina said, "I do not know as one's destiny is within and ours is not. We must go. This place is half a day's journey away."

They got ready and gathered the last of needed items, Salina doing most of this since Laura had no idea what to get. Now once everything's together, they began.

CHAPTER

twenty-eight

The things that were in the bag Laura had no clue as to what they were. She just followed Salina. One thing did catch her wonder though, "Why so much tea?"

"Oh, well, I like it and everyone needs a habit. Mine's tea," Salina said with a smile.

"We, in the old days, would have walked or taken a wagon, but today, we drive and it is so much nicer on one's feet!" Salina said with a laugh, maybe to lighten up the mood of what they were facing. Now almost to the pile that blocked the town, Salina looked at Laura and asked, "You do have the keys, yes?" Searching the small pack that she had, Laura reached in and brought out her keys with a jingle.

"Yep, right here."

Filling the car with the bags they entered and now there was no turning back. Wishing she could know how to get to places as Salina (with no maps or directions), Laura waited for the instructions. As the drive went, Laura seen more and more of this lovely country-side and she caught herself really liking—no, falling in love with the beauty and simplicity of it. She heard Salina say, "Follow these woods until you see the stones of a once magnificent home that once stood there. Then, at the tower, follow the left side to the cliff." Salina said she would not get lost, as these were nothing to miss.

Driving in silence and driving with only scenery, Laura began thinking or asking again why. Shaking this feeling, she looked more at the road as to not have chicken fever. Salina sipped on her tea as she has done shortly after the start of the engine, spoke up and now getting over and beyond the directions she had given, she said, "Yes, to answer your question. Yes, it was a very pretty and welcoming home, with lots of smiles and children about." Then she said something that almost made Laura stop the car and freak out. "This was the home of the Cordley Clan. They owned all the land that you can see when we reach the top, and then some. When the shame came, it was not just Curtis but his whole family name. They left not even to sell any because people were afraid. To this day, no one has claimed any and the state has taken care for it as long as I can remember."

Laura turned and now applying the brakes asked, "No one has ever asked to buy?"

"No, because they are told the stories and get scared and don't buy."

"Wow, that's strange. It is so beautiful up here!"

"Aye, it is but to what price?" This was the last Salina spoke of the home and lands except for a sharp "Head to the water's edge."

Doing as she was told, Laura slightly turned and headed the way she was directed. She started to feel a pulling sensation in her stomach and something else she could not put her finger on. Silence between them again, but the closer the car got, the more intense the feeling was and Salina looked over to Laura.

"Ye, can feel him can ye, child? The feeling of want."

"Yes, I can. I have never felt this before, but yes, I can feel something."

"It is him. You are close now to where he lays. Still I know not the exact lair. We still have one more thing to do and then I will know where."

"How?"

"You shall see." Coming up from a small gully area of brownish green grass to see in the distance nothing but water as far as your eyes could focus, Laura looked in shock. This was the same color as her dreams, and the closer she drove, a shape came into view. A lonely tree at the end of the cliff, the tree that he and her made love under the first time. Laura's heart was racing now and she knew Salina also knew without needing to hear it.

Closer and closer then Salina said, "Stop, right there before the tree." Getting out and gesturing Laura to do so also, not before being asked to retrieve the bag that she had brought. Laura did and hastened to follow her to where she had stopped. With a twinkle in her eyes as if she was into mischief, Salina asked Laura to help make a picnic area, as she was hungry. Laura did and remembered that this scene looked a lot like her dream. "Let's sit and eat a bite before we begin." Both sitting and Salina getting things from the bag, which had sandwiches, chips, and small bits of cheese, and a few drinks, Laura took the portion that was given and waited for Salina to get hers then they ate in silence, just looking out over the magnificent view.

Almost done Salina took out from her bag a container holding some kind of liquid and poured each of them a small amount. "What's this?" asked Laura.

Smiling Salina replied, "It will help us on our journey. Now drink, child." She drank until the last drop and finishing asked, "Now what?"

"We wait," Salina said quietly.

Waiting didn't take long but maybe a half hour or so because Laura started to feel very sluggish, as if she had taken a tranquilizer or something. She started to panic. "What have you done, given me?" she shouted to Salina.

"It will not harm you but will bring on the dream plane he come to you in. Now sleep, child, and go to him." She watched as Laura slowly drifted into a comatose state. Salina prepared for what had to be done. She had to do it quickly because as Laura went her work began. Watching closely Salina waited for just the right time.

Laura, now in her dream, first noticed herself right where there were but Salina was not there nor was anything else. Not the blanket, food, or even the car. "Holy fuck," she spoke out loud except at that moment there was a form in the corner of her eyes' vision. Catching her breath and not being able to speak due to shock, it was he standing now in front of her leaning against the tree. "I knew we would be together, you and I, my love!"

Laura now found her voice. "But how?" He walked over to her, and as he bent down in front of her, he was close enough that his face brushed against hers, and in that moment, he saw fear that was not there before. Or was it desire? He did not know. The latter was what he wanted so he kissed her with so much passion Laura thought she was going to float away. The kiss was endless and his hands now moved over her breasts on top of her coat and shirt then slowly down to where he pulled her top out so his left hand could go under the clothing then the other hand. Laura bent her chest into his larger palms as they still kissed. He laid her down by easing their bodies together still in the kiss and his hands holding her breast in such splendor. Giving up his right hand, he unbuttoned her jeans and pushed his hand into the opening between her body and the cloth, down through her soft curls and between the already moistened and swollen lips already on the verge. He entered with two long center fingers of his hand. Laura's body jumped as he pushed then into her in one push.

She and he were both breathing heavily. He broke the kiss, releasing their lips with a smack and an "ahhh" from Laura. Taking his fingers out of her so both hands could push her pants down, he made her naked from the waist down. Once her pants were off, his fingers entered again with a tremendous orgasm coming from deep inside. His fingers stilled as Laura's muscles spasm then he opened her legs and placed his head between the thighs, spreading her with his tongue, swiping over her throbbing female flower. He licked savagely then where his wetted fingers were his tongue entered over them and he licked her, as she was the sweetest candy. He brought her into another sensation of heaven. Swallowing her juices and playing his fingers inside her to where he could go no further. Taking his fingers out to undress himself and still on his knees and between her thighs, he stood and, standing there, took his heavy shaft to place it just to her opening. Now taking his hands and holding her to bend her back and lift her shirt to make her now completely naked as he kissed her body. Then he entered her. She bucked her hips when his penis went into her all the way with one thrust until their hips were grinding together. Entering and pulling out until only the head was inside, he repeated this motion again and again and again until he felt her grasping him for another release. His own swelling inside and feeling his balls tightening he knew this was to be together and they would fly. One last hard push into her as fast and deep as he could do, he released at the same time with Laura, holding him inside.

Curtis held his body above Laura's with only the strength of his arms and legs. His knees finally were giving out and he released the suction that held them together. Opening his eyes and looking straight ahead, he went from ecstasy to rage in one blink because, standing there no more than five feet was the old woman from the other day. Looking directly into her eyes, Curtis screamed in an inhuman voice, "Woman, yea shall regret interfering in my business!" Rising up and leaving Laura there to watch, he stood naked and in a movement toward Salina so quick the normal eye could not see, yet Salina was not the norm. He moved then stood waiting for something, then he moved again, getting closer and closer until he was within reach of Salina. Raising her hand in the form of a fist, she waited for him to come nearer, and turning the fist into an opened hand, she blew. A cloud of powdery substance went forth and wrapped around Curtis as if he took two ears and smacked them together. This was no ordinary powder, and she spoke, "Now is done, is from this moment you are as you were."

Not thinking it was anything but just a powder and an old woman, Curtis went straight for her throat, slicing it with his elongated thumbnail. Unfortunately, he didn't notice the long bone-handled knife she held, which she held tight in his chest. Each looking at each other's eyes, knowing one or both would not survive. Curtis released her throat to grab hold of the knife that now would not come out of its place deep within his heart. For hundreds of years, he has not suffered from colds, cuts, heat, or blizzards, and now a frail old woman has done what nature and demon hounds have not. She, by means of gypsy magic, made his spirit corporeal again and has killed him with the only thing that could—his own knife made from the bone of the very person he himself murdered so many, many years ago. As the confrontation between them was happening, Laura came aware at the moment the knife plunged his heart, as if it was her own and all she could do was watch with her eyes. She couldn't even move until Curtis vanished, leaving Salina with an opened neck. Then she also vanished. Next thing Laura saw was the green blue waters of the sea and Salina lying on the ground half dead with her hands around her neck. Rushing to her side, Laura's body still slightly numb, she grabbed the blanket and wrapped it around the neck of this woman who, by all means, saved her. With a look in her eyes Salina stared at Laura with love and something else, relief. Then, she was gone.

Tears running down her face, she picked up the old woman, not knowing where the strength came from and placed her into the car leaving everything behind. Driving all that day back to where Salina's home was and again picking her up and carrying her through the town, onto the trail falling many times to her knees she followed that path leading to her home. Arriving at the house she opened the door and placed her into the chair she sat in, taking sometime and wishing she knew what to do. Then she saw a note in the seat of the place that she herself laid in. Picking it up, shaking, she carefully opened it and read,

If you live and I do not, place me in my chair, take my book, and keep it safe. Then burn my home. I am with my family now and not of any need of this no more.

Laura read this and, with all she has been through now, didn't think twice to do as she wished. Somehow the book had come back to the house without her retrieving it from the cliff. She picked it up.

The last thing Laura saw before getting into the car was a bright orange glow over the treetops and she drove up the mountain ever reminded when she looked into the review mirror.

five years later

Married and heavy with child, Laura was now living in Ireland, the land she fell in love with and also a tall dark-haired Irish man by the name Doland whom she met on the plane back to the States after what she calls her life's journey.

Standing with him and watching the workman clear off the old homestead that once stood on this ground they each were summoned to come see a discovery that was unearthed. Running over and looking into the hole that once was the entrance to its walls was the bone of a human, but that wasn't what made them unusual. Staring at them Laura's blood stilled in her body because there in this hole with the bones was a knife sticking out of what would have been its chest.

A bone-handled blade.

Paths of each of our destinies crisscross through life. Only death will set the ghosts free.

about the author

Andrea Stryker is a free spirit who lives in North Florida with her husband. Never in all her dreams would she have imagined one of her stories would be in print, but with encouragement from a couple of her (six) children, their spouses, and close friends, she took that chance.

Starting life in the south west and growing up in the Midwest until she became a tender mid-teenager and found her way to the southeast and finding her life mate, she began a family that has grown now into having a never-quiet home of dogs and grandchildren, yet she wouldn't change a thing!

Writing has always been a passion but living and learning always come first. Still working a full-time job, she took a moment to take a chance. She hopes all who reads her book(s) enjoys it as much as she did writing them. Always keep reading as reading is knowledge.

CPSIA information can be obtained
at www.ICGtesting.com
Printed in the USA
FSHW020420261019
63402FS